Nova Hellas

Stories from Future Greece

Edited by Francesca T Barbini & Francesco Verso

Luna Press
PUBLISHING

First published by Luna Press Publishing, Edinburgh, 2021

The following stories first appered in the following publications:

'Roseweed' Vasso Christou. *a2525: Stories from future Athens, 2017.*
'Social Engineering' Kostas Charitos. *a2525: Stories from future Athens, 2017.*
'The Human(c)ity of Athens' Ioanna Bourazopoulou. *a2525: Stories from future Athens, 2017.*
'Bagdad Square' Michalis Manolios. *a2525: Stories from future Athens, 2017.*
'The Bee Problem' Yannis Papadopoulos & Stamatis Stamatopoulos. *a2525: Stories from future Athens, 2017.*
'T2' Kelly Theodorakopoulou. *a2525: Stories from future Athens, 2017.*
'Those We Serve' Eugenia Triantafyllou. *Interzone, Issue 287, May 2020.*
'Abacos' Lina Theodorou. *a2525: Stories from future Athens, 2017.*
'Any old desease' Dimitra Nikolaidou. *Metaphorosis, March 2018.*
'Android whores can't cry' Natalia Theodoridou. *Clarkesworld Magazine, Issue 106, July 2015.*
'The Colour that Defines Me' Stamatis Stamatopoulos. *Εφαρμοσμένη Μυθομηχανική, 2014.*

_____

The following stories have been translated by:

Dimitra Nikolaidou and Vaya Pseftaki for
'Roseweed'
'Social Engineering'
'The Human(c)ity of Athens'
'The Bee Problem'
'Baghdad Square'
'T2'
'Abacos'

Stephanie Polakis for
'The Colour that defines me'

www.lunapresspublishing.com
ISBN-13: 978-1-913387-37-2

Contents

Introduction
Dimitra Nikolaidou   vi

Roseweed
Vasso Christou   1

Social Engineering
Kostas Charitos   14

The Human(c)ity of Athens
Ioanna Bourazopoulou   28

Baghdad Square
Michalis Manolios   40

The Bee Problem
Yiannis Papadopoulos & Stamatis Stamatopoulos 53

T2
Kelly Theodorakopoulou   66

Those We Serve
Eugenia Triantafyllou   75

Abacos
Lina Theodorou   92

Any Old Disease
Dimitra Nikolaidou   96

Android Whores Can't Cry
Natalia Theodoridou   113

The Colour that Defines Me
Stamatis Stamatopoulos   131

Contributors   149

Introduction

Space travel, alien encounters and interplanetary wars: Lucian's True Story (Ἀληθῆ Διηγήματα) had it all. Written in the 2nd century AD, this ancient Greek text is still considered to be the first work of science fiction; it certainly provided the narrative blueprints for centuries to come.

However, despite these illustrious beginnings, science fiction took a long time to establish itself in Greece; it wasn't until 1929 that Dimosthenis Voutyras published *From Earth to Mars* (Ἀπό τη Γη Στον Ἄρη), the first Greek science fiction work to come after Lucian's True Story. A few more titles by a handful of authors followed Voutyras' work over the next ten years, but the turbulent political situation, which persisted until the early '80s, did not allow for the proliferation of the genre. Greek fiction was firmly focussed on political or social issues; the fantastical element was mostly limited to children's stories and folk tales. Greek myths might have inspired many seminal speculative authors abroad, but fantasy, science fiction, and horror weren't particularly popular in the country itself, at least until the '70s: Dr Domna Pastourmatzi, professor of American Literature at Aristotle University, who specialises in science fiction, notes that, in the sixties, only eleven science fiction novels and one anthology had been translated into Greek.

However, this was soon to change for two reasons: the fall of the military dictatorship in 1974, and the reestablishment of democracy, brought a desire to explore new, previously censored and neglected genres; furthermore, the success of *Star Wars*, and of TV series like *Star Trek*, finally turned the attention of authors and audience towards science fiction. In the beginning, it was pulp that came to the rescue: paperback translations and cheap anthologies mainly sold at street kiosks introduced the canon of speculative fiction to the public for the first time. By the end of that decade, and going into the eighties, small publishing houses began to translate contemporary classics such as Ursula le Guin and Isaac Asimov, and finally introducing them to actual bookshops, thus helping to set up a scene of dedicated fans. However, even as hundreds of novels and short stories were published in a few short years, the critics reacted unfavourably to the explosion of science fiction, which they derided as (to quote Dr Pastourmatzi again) "American Paraliterature." The newly founded science fiction scene kept a relatively low profile, supported by zines, a few dedicated magazines, and a few daring publishers.

In the late '90s-early 2000s, things had begun to quickly change. The advent of the internet surely played a part. Equally important, though, was the publication of 9 magazine, which was included in the major *Eleftherotypia* newspaper every Wednesday. While focussing mainly on comics, 9 also published a short story every week, either in Greek or translated, thus providing speculative writers with a mainstream outlet as well as familiarising the general public with the genre. Soon, more writers felt encouraged to write speculative fiction, and dedicated groups formed, which still remain influential today.

\#

ALEF (the Science Fiction Club of Athens) was formed in 1998; the editor of 9, Aggelos Mastorakis, was the first president as well as one of the founding members. In 1999, ALEF began organising yearly writing workshops, which were soon to become biannual; in 2003, ALEF began publishing *Fantastika Chronika* (*Φαντασικά Χρονικά*) which, to this day, remains the longest published Greek science fiction magazine.

Science fiction fans, and readers of genre fiction in general, were no longer keeping a low profile. In 2003, the sff.gr forum allowed writers and fans of speculative fiction to gather in one large community for the first time. By then, the success of The Lord of the Rings movie trilogy, as well as the introduction of MMORPGs, was beginning to introduce speculative works into the mainstream, and science fiction benefitted from that development as much as fantasy did. A few dedicated publishing houses now focussed on speculative fiction, including novels from Greek authors, along with Greek anthologies in their publishing programme. ALEF's workshops produced two anthologies, while its members went on to establish themselves through their individual works.

It was the visual artist Lina Theodorou who called upon ALEF's authors to imagine a future Athens, in the context of the 2017 exhibition titled "Tomorrows", initially presented in Onassis Stegi in that same year. The collaboration between visual artists and authors resulted in the book *a2525: Stories from a Future Athens* (2017). In the years to come, *a2525* would be translated into the English (as *Nova Hellas*, Luna Press Publishing) and Italian languages (Future Fiction), enriched with even more stories from Greek authors, and finally become the book you're currently holding.

#

What makes this book uniquely Greek? After all, as seen above, the science fiction genre took a long time to finally return and be accepted back into its birthplace. Can we claim that Greek science fiction has already found a voice of its own?

The answer came to us as we were translating many of the stories from Greek to English, and quickly noticed a pattern. Given our turbulent history, and the fact that *a2525* was written during a harsh economic crisis, it comes as no surprise that most authors within have imagined a rather dystopian future, and envisioned harsh times to come. And yet, as pessimistic as these visions of the future might be, their protagonists turn out to be remarkably resilient. Cunning and resourceful, they decide to not only survive but thrive, no matter the circumstances. They stealthily make the stories optimistic through sheer will, almost stubbornly working against the pessimistic visions of their own creators. In doing so, they reflect both the history of Greece itself, always surviving and rebuilding, always claiming a better tomorrow – and, perhaps, to a smaller degree, the stubbornness of Greek science fiction, which insisted on thriving in adverse circumstances and against much opposition (be that military dictators or dismissive critics). As such, this anthology emerges as a portrait not only of a future, imaginary Greece, but as the depiction of a continuous rebirth process, burning bright even as it deceptively casts itself in shadows.

Dimitra Nikolaidou

Roseweed
Vasso Christou

Translators from Greek: Dimitra Nikolaidou, Vaya Pseftaki

Thirty three minutes to go.

Each and every time she swore it wouldn't happen to her, yet each time that moment came when Alba began to stress out. At approximately forty minutes of oxygen left, possible catastrophes were parading through her mind: flashlight malfunction, oxygen supply system lockup, an earthquake. The latest addition was the threat of 'Residence Quality', this mysterious activist group that trapped the foundations of submerged buildings when least expected. All right. What kind of residence quality did anyone expect in a building, when its entrance was six meters under dirty water? Alba had walked around the crowded camps at the foothills of Mount Aigaleo. She had an informed opinion on the quality of life of those who did *not* possess a residence any more.

Two exploded buildings, without any victims truth be told. Her deep breath sent the bubbles upwards. *This building would not be a trapped one.* She passed carefully through the remnants of the glass door, and entered the room which, according to the old blueprints, used to be an office. She shed her light across the wall opposite her, where one of the main pillars climbed upwards. Some torn posters swung in the current her movements had set forth. A heavy curtain that hadn't dissolved yet, let tittles of light distill themselves inside the room. She passed over a large piece of furniture that used to be a desk—it seemed heavy, made of solid wood, really impossible to lift. Clumps of red and black seaweed stirred out of the drawer cracks. In such places, only this mutant Gulf seaweed thrived. The water was way too unwelcoming to fish and seashells.

Most buildings had been thoroughly evacuated when the rise of the water levels forced Piraeus' residents to wave their port goodbye. Abandoned valuables spoke either of too much sorrow, or of too much wealth. The building on Mavromichali street used to belong to a shipping company. One of the first to move their main offices to safe ground.

Another deep breath. *It won't happen to me. Nothing will happen to me.* She steadied one hand with another and stuck the drill inside the pillar, to get to the last wall sample. It was not the lack of oxygen, she told herself. Her forced severance from the information network had gone from the stage of simple irritation to the first withdrawal symptoms. The curtain oscillated gently along the vibrations of the impact drill. Twenty-six minutes. Still. She had extracted ten samples. If the foundations were trapped, the mechanisms would have been triggered by now. The buzz of the drill steadily increased the beating of her heart.

Nothing bad will happen.

*

The lugger containing their equipment, tied to the balustrade of the building's second floor, was violently rocking. The wind had picked up during her dive. Alba activated her connection to the information network the minute she removed the diving regulator. Hakim's hands extended, first to pick up the sack of samples and then her, along with the scuba tanks. The newsfeeds from dozens of meteorological stations from all over the world downloaded updates for the most important weather events. Cataclysmic floods in Naples—the service had predicted those days ago—, typhoon scale winds in the Philippines, a sandstorm in Tripoli—she backtracked as she grabbed the rail. In Libya or in Peloponnesus? These last years, given the draught in the Arcadian Plateau, it was not outside the realm of possibility. As she got back to the news, the red envelope containing the urgent messages blinked in the upper right corner and started enlarging itself, till it covered half her right eye.

Libya. Alba rode over the rail, closing her eyes for a moment. She did not stop seeing the notification, of course. The implant sent the information straight to her retina. All she managed to shut out was the rainbow hue of the oil stain, through which she had emerged. The scant oil remaining in the flooded tanks was still finding its way to the surface, years after the event. She accepted the message as she left the diving assistant to take the heavy equipment off her back. It was from the head engineer.

I will take care of the samples.

She wrinkled her brows while taking her gloves off in a hurry, in order to lift her hair before Hakim completely removed her hood. Under no circumstances did she want to allow her auburn braid to touch the wet suit. Apart from the oil, the grey and green waters stank of eutrophic microorganisms, rotten seaweed, garbage and dirt.

For the third time in just a few weeks, Balatsas was asking to personally check the samples Alba had removed from the load-bearing elements. Did he have any reason not to trust in her work? In their four years of cooperation, she had never heard of a client complaint. Obviously, someone was paying a lot of money so the building could get a higher suitability rating. But Alba knew her employer to be almost legit; he only toyed with the footnotes, attributing, in his certificates, no more than one degree of suitability higher than he was supposed to, at most. Not to mention that in this game, he had made them all partners and accomplishes. If the state considered the load-bearing capacity of submerged flats good enough, who would say no to a few extra cents?

'Water?'

Alba took big gulps out of the bottle the Syrian assistant was offering to her, while looking absent-mindedly at the sack's pockets, bulging with samples. The experience of so many years was telling her that this building would have no problem getting an 'adequate residence' certificate. Why would Balatsas want the samples?

Hakim pointed towards the upper floor. 'How long will you

take inside?'

The waves from the old port moved towards Dragatsaniou street; first unveiling the stained marble of the veranda, then forcefully covering them, throwing seaweed on the walls of the second floor. They had altered roseweed to eat away the oil, but it multiplied exponentially instead, thriving on the waste. Alba squinted and looked at the oily waters swelling rhythmically up to the new beach, near the Saint Sophia church. Two small passenger boats bobbed near Papastratou street, tied up in re-inhabited flats.

Flooding in Nepal and predictions of strong whirlwinds in Massachusetts. She lowered the news flow by two clicks. Outside the water she was allowed to access the network, but there was still a lot of work to be done. If she was not late, nobody would suspect she had picked one or two superfluous samples.

'About an hour.'

'Shitty weather,' Hakim murmured pulling the tanks over to the stirring wheel.

Which means 'hurry up.' She nodded. In Ravenna they were urgently re-enforcing the sea walls, to face the upcoming weather. Maybe not closing off Gibraltar when they still had time was a mistake on the Europeans' part. They said the Mediterranean Sea would die off. As if it was alive now, she snorted, scrunching her nose against the all-encompassing stench.

*

The lugger stopped bobbing as it navigated the ring of the former Peace and Friendship Stadium, leaving the naked tips of the submerged trees behind. They were past the shadow of the breakwater. Every time they arrived there, she remembered diving with her first boyfriend in the flooded tunnel that led to the Phaliro train station by the stadium, back when they heightened and reinforced the groyne day and night. She also remembered the beating they had taken once their parents found out.

When she was a child, her parents used to curse their fate. They had come to Greece from Durrës as minors seeking a better tomorrow, worked themselves to the bone, and then ended up with children of their own, trapped in a foreign country which crumbled financially. Nobody took the scenarios of overheating and water level rises seriously. Lots of computer models, lots of protocols for the elimination of pollution, lots of talking for best and worst case scenarios—nothing said of the waters rising more than one or two meters by the end of the century. Until the Siberia and Antarctica incidents proved how much there was still to learn about the planet, how vulnerable the cities were and how arrogantly ignorant were the ones responsible. The first year round, it was twenty centimeters. And then, six meters in the next five years. It took three more years for fifty more centimeters, and after that the situation seemed to stabilize itself in a world that did not have enough time to protect its cities, while struggling at the same time with a wave of refugees, famine, plagues, panic and rabid fanaticism. Alba was watching the temperature and weather broadcast throughout her entire adolescence. It was her nightmarish escape from the scared talk of her parents, who expected to be at some point the victims of the up and coming 'Pure Greece' movement. Pakistanis, Syrians and Africans were constant targets—as if they were the ones that made the waters rise. Albanians were very white, long in the country, they had adapted better. They slipped through.

Alba jumped on the cement brim of the pier at Karaiskaki Stadium, the company's anchorage. It was Hakim's job to guard their equipment. She would wait for the lift to take her to the Kastela office. In Ravenna, the army was brought in to drop rapid-setting cement. She hugged the heavy sample bag closer. Why had the head engineer become so greedy all of a sudden? After all, she was the one who needed to buy an extra hour of air conditioning in the summer. He could use it all day long.

*

'Did they swamp you?' Tasos asked when he reached the door.

'Nah. I myself arranged to draft the reports now, so I won't have to come in at all tomorrow.'

'Ah, sure,' he guffawed getting out. 'Your day off. I imagine Tafari, that angel of a man, will let you spend it on a wild night, bent over diagrams.'

Alba shook her head at nothing. The well-known joke had been tossed around for so long, it was not funny anymore. Tasos had admitted he was jealous that the law forced employers to give half a day off for every two four-hour dives. But his aggression did not derive so much from her hard-earned day, as from the notion that she spent it doing assignments and studying for her second degree. Since it was not making her money, it was useless. Period.

Her mother had prevented her from studying meteorology. Her argument was unshakable: if the daughter of a cleaning lady wanted to get ahead in life, she had to pursue studies in a field where demand was high. As the waters rose, so rose the need for engineers. The Greek government, constantly in the throes of a crisis, never managed to coordinate itself and protect the coastal cities the way most other countries had done. However, the demand for civil engineers still increased, for other reasons. Those trained in diving and daring enough to submerge themselves in the dangerous labyrinths of the underwater basements, were quite sought after. Alba had managed to crawl into that market niche. In spite of her mother though, she had not chosen the work for the money, but for the days off, which she used to study meteorology. Studies she had to pay for.

Three of her assignments were due this week, yet the reason she stayed at the office late was not the forthcoming day off. Though she did not dare search through Balatsas' archives to see exactly what was going on with the samples, she could still look at the warehouse where the cylinders were classified and examine them herself.

She had to correct her report multiple times. She was nervous, and paid for that nervousness with more time than she had planned to. To be prepared for every occasion, she connected to the university website and downloaded the assignments. If she was discovered staying for more than it was reasonable, at worst she would be reprimanded for spending the company's electricity for personal reasons, nothing more.

She entered the head engineer's office without turning on the light. She liked going near the big window at night, the one with the view of Phaliro and Moschato. In the darkness, she could make out neither the submerged buildings nor the grey waters that had made an island out of Peiraiki. Only some scattered lights—buildings that had been deemed suitable for habitation—on the Non-land. She groped in the dark and found the keys by the locker. Scattered thoughts of those who could only live in the half-submerged blocks, moving around in boats over the poisonous roseweed or setting makeshift bridges between the higher balconies, chased themselves around her mind. The boarders signed away their right to be rescued in the case of a collapse no matter the cause. As she had signed hers right away, so she would get hired. The next big earthquake... she shivered.

She clutched the key in her hand, her eyes still nailed on the dark outskirts between land and Non-land, the citizens and the pariahs. Steadily, she took it out of the key locker.

*

One by one, the photovoltaic arrays on the railings went out, leaving the turbulent waters under the bridges dark in the time between night and dawn. She was a bit cold, from the day's exhaustion and the night's sleeplessness, but she also welcomed the northern wind that drove away, even for a little while, the seaweed stench around her. When she was a child, the November winds were at their coldest at that hour.

She used to go back home on the little trams that connected, over the low metal bridges, the island of Peiraiki with the Moschato station. That dawn, she had chosen to walk instead, to empty her head from the night's thoughts, so as not to see samples and reports before her eyes when she finally crawled into bed. She had to jump over a motionless body, curled up on the stairs of the last bridge. Tafari would tell her off for going around on foot at this hour. Athens had become more dangerous than the Ethiopia his parents had abandoned, long before he was born. Him being a civil engineer, responsible for one of the numerous construction sites at Phaliro's new gurnoys, did make him a bit more optimistic—but only a little bit. Anything dangerous raised his old insecurities to the surface. 'Pure Greece' never stopped threatening whoever seemed different. On him, the difference was obvious.

The watch on her retina showed 06:27. She quickened her

step to get to him before he left for work. She didn't know if there was any point telling him what she had discovered at this early hour, but her partner was a good listener, and she wanted to unload somewhere.

All the samples they had gathered and that Balatsas had taken from them, suggested that buildings were obviously safe, according to the criteria established by the Ministry of Physical Planning. However, every building she had examined in the last two months—all of them behind the Electric Train Station, towards Drapetsona—, had been characterized by the head engineer as next to last in terms of suitability. Any recently published decree, would have judged them to be suitable for demolition only. Not that anybody cared to demolish the Non-land. A thorough search at the Ministry's archives for those certificates issued during the last months in the area, informed her that other technical companies had also certified buildings in the area as non-suitable for residence, or for any other use.

Even statistically speaking, this was improbable.

Three large screens at the electric train station broadcasted the news to the few passengers that had no implants. Alba turned her attention from the unrest in London to the news she already knew about. At Ravenna, one of the dams had collapsed and the victims numbered up to three thousands already. They had fooled the sea only for so long. The foul weather was rapidly advancing east. Perhaps the Greeks were better after all, folding their cards against the sea before the battle had even begun?

Why would anyone want to deem buildings that fulfilled the safety criteria, as uninhabitable? Perhaps it was another trick of 'Residence Quality' to discourage re-habitation? Yet, if the mysterious protectors of the organization had enough money to bribe the engineers, why not take it a step further and bribe directly the ones who issued decrees on the criteria? Reasons of conscience were much less likely to be detected. And after all, why not pay to set up climate refugees in other places? With real residence quality?

Dirty business, Tafari would say. Stay away. All right. Everybody knew that. Old shops in the square around Kapodistriou street had become the best drug dealing dens. It was easy for the small speedboats to move between the buildings. The labyrinth of the apartment blocks hid them from prying eyes on both land and sea, and the old balconies shielded them even from the satellites. But no. Substances are traded in grams. No drug dealing business needs so much space. Human organs? They would need cryo-cooling installations, and electric companies did not supply the Non-land. Anything there functioned on generators only. So, no...

Alba tightened her jacket around her as she entered the station. Tafari would warn her not to get involved. She smiled. She was not one to dive in dangerous buildings, and yet be scared away from an internet search.

*

'Hydra Park? Hydra Park what?'

'This is the name of the company that owns every building from Kondyli beach and beyond the old Jumbo warehouses, down to the Papastratos border. They bought those through a Swiss construction company. They're based on Maryland.'

The sun was setting red in the West, dying the dead seaweed rocking under the recently constructed pier purple. The foul weather wave had drowned more than six thousand people in Ravenna and it was crossing the Adriatic, but it would reach the Ionian weakened. Alba shielded her eyes as she looked at her tall partner who had his back on the calm sea. 'All these falsified certificates are issued on their behalf. The company has bought everything before even checking them—which is not the standard procedure.'

'Then, HydraPark didn't ask them to falsify the certificates so they can buy cut-price buildings?' Tafari asked.

'It wouldn't have been to their interest, since certificates have a ten-year duration and you have to go through the courts to correct them after the issue. They could not make use of them easily with a classification like that, and my boss would not risk losing the Ministry's sanction.' Yesterday's wind had quieted and if the stillness didn't make the air so foul, Alba would have taken a deep breath. 'The company's site is asking for divers no matter their specialty. Part time and full time.'

'OK,' Tafari said haltingly, his eyebrows meeting over worried eyes. 'Then no matter what it is that they do, they at least function within the limits of the law, at least in part.'

'I hope so,' she said, taking that breath after all. 'Because ten minutes after my last search, they messaged me. They want to see me.'

She could swear that Tafari went pale under his dark skin.

*

'A theme park? You want to build a theme park, offering rides in Piraeus' abandoned buildings?'

'What else?' said the interviewer, her voice so jovial you would think all she knew of life was the fun to be had in such parks. 'Virtual reality has kept people occupied for a few years, but since it became available to everyone, all our well-off customers prefer the live experience. We offer them a dangerous trip through ghost cities.'

'What do you mean exactly?'

The PR specialist—Alba's full CV, which she had never sent herself, glowing on her tablet—gestured theatrically, touching her heart over her white shirt. 'Oh, unfortunately, entertainment requires danger, Ms Gatse. It takes adrenaline to win your customer over.'

'But the buildings are not really dangerous.'

Her eyes sparkled. 'The buildings have genuine certificates stating that every activity inside them is potentially dangerous. This way, we're offering a unique opportunity to those who want to experience something special!'

'So, you will set up restaurants and casinos on the upper floors. Well-sealed, so the stench doesn't cause retching, I assume.'

'That's the least of it. We're setting up escape rooms. On time limit. You cannot exit, no matter the danger. We're talking about the experience of a lifetime!'

'And what will the divers do? Strengthen the foundations?'

'A wonderful idea, Ms Gatse. I'm thinking of suggesting your recruitment not on a part-time, but on a full-time basis, if you so desire.'

'I don't have much time. I'm working on a second degree, but you already know that, don't you?'

A big, pseudo-friendly smile crawled on her lips. 'Of course. Weather news are not good enough for you, are they, dear Alba? You will allow me the informality, won't you? You want to foresee the events *before* they come to be. You are not among those who can sit back and helplessly watch the flooding. You want to intervene. And trust me,' her voice lowered in an imitation of confidentiality, 'you can.'

Pretty powerful PR studies, Alba thought while the woman carried on. 'You have time to think about it. There are plenty of positions. The initial duty of the divers will be to decorate fully and in every detail the underwater places. Then, we'll need tour guides.'

'The water is heavily polluted. And it brims with poisonous seaweed.'

'But of course.' The hologram of a two-seater microsubmarine popped in front of her in three dimensions, almost real. 'This is why we chose, for this particular tour, buildings with large doors and balcony exits. Most will have a comfortable, protected round of the living rooms and the office complexes' lobbies.'

Alba heard what was coming before she was told. Diving equipment, similar to hers but shinier, filled the space at the side. 'But, those who want to live the grand experience, those who want to go through the anxiety, the bitterness and the danger, will have to pay a bit more. How will they be able to say, down the course of their life, that they escaped the rooms of a possibly trapped and certified dangerous basement under polluted waters? Or, for the more cultured ones, that they got their hands on a book soaking for years in a submerged library?'

*

Alba activated the keyboard.

Explain Horrid Picture

Communications with the surface were a luxury she didn't have in her normal job, but here it was necessary, for the more effective decoration of the flooded rooms.

'Recreation of the damage water does on the face,' said the ever-jovial voice.

I've seen. Water not damages images this way

'Ah, forget you are an engineer, Alba.' Always with the aggressively friendly and confidential attitude. 'This is show business. It matters not what the water does. What is important, is scaring the client. They're here for the adrenaline; you must take it to new heights. They'll enter the bedroom in the half-light. A pinch of horror is part of the game. This is what our psychologists advise, after reviewing the profiles of thousands of possible clients.'

So many rich people, so many *stupid* rich people, who want to spend their time in buildings considered dangerous, so many cannibals who want to feed by invading the misery of those who abandoned their houses when the seas claimed them. Fold. HydraPark was paying well. Every two dives, one more hour of air conditioning for a month.

Forty minutes to go. She kicked upwards to the ceiling. Plenty of time to secure the curtains. If only she could float in her home too, when she had to hang them on the windows.

Not enough time left to place the pots and pans in the kitchen, so as to give the necessary dramatic touch. She needed a lot of fine work there to make everything seem right. On her next day off from Balatsas and his certificates.

She checked the oxygen index again, once she was done with the curtain rails. Thirty four minutes to go. Enough time to worry. Flashlight malfunction, no—she didn't work here alone anymore. The guys underneath her now placed a mattress on the bed's wooden frame, held on the floor by weights. Through the seaweed clumps, she could discern them aligning it to the corners. Damage to the oxygen supply system, no—they had time enough to help her to the surface. Earthquake. This... this was always a possibility. But with HydraPark, she hadn't signed away her rescue rights.

The mattress started filling, and it sat heavily on the frame when her colleagues tore the plastic wrapping. She could spot a couple of indelible stains from above. Perfect. Plausibility achieved with garbage as the raw material. Some were preparing the relevant tall-tales they would later spin during the underwater tours.

The threat of explosives had been stricken off the list. It was only a trick of the company, a foreshadowed sense of danger. At some point, a truly unsuitable building would collapse. A very discreet team was taking care of it. One or two microexplosions as the show went on would throw adrenaline off the charts, adding the spice of real danger. And if one of those idiot millionaires was so scared they dropped dead, she didn't give a damn. The game was made for exactly this group of people that had flooded them with seaweed and shit. Plus, the total IQ of humanity would increase, by the tiniest fraction.

She carefully grabbed two handfuls of roseweed with her gloved hands and started weaving them through the holes in the tattered curtains, a sort of special effect. *Thirty minutes.* She laughed and the bubbles travelled upwards.

Seaweed sold as silken ribbons. That's what it was.

Social Engineering
Kostas Charitos

Translators from Greek: Dimitra Nikolaidou, Vaya Pseftaki

'What is a problem? Something you cannot solve on your own? Wrong. A problem is something you think someone else can solve.'

I stand on the edge of the stone precipice, looking at the long, blazing river that flows in front of the Panathenaic Stadium. The light reflects on the bleachers, making the Pentelic marble glow orange. The stadium seems like a huge restart button, inviting you to push it, to tear the whole city down and rebuild it from scratch.

'You know what really gets on my nerves?' I ask the angel fluttering next to me, but he doesn't respond. Maybe they've upgraded the Augmented Reality function, to get rhetorical questions.

'That everyone thinks I'm the asshole who's going to solve their problems.'

'It is not right to use such language, my child,' the angel says.

'What's this river of fire doing in the middle of Athens?'

'A reminder of the fate of mankind. The everlasting fire, awaiting the sinners.'

I'm curious whether the Greek Church paid the company that developed the software for them, or if some believer has donated it for free. Anyhow, if they spent even one micro-bitcoin on this winged thing that talks like my village preacher, then they were certainly taken for a ride.

'I was thinking of finding a place to chill for a bit,' I say and Athens' temples flash like lights on a Christmas tree.

'Somewhere where I could drink some Isabella-grape tsipouro,' I clarify. The angel performs a theatrical move with his good wing, a curve that turns off the temples and lights up the coffeehouses instead. There's a special offer on tsipouro in a small coffee shop, near Karytsi street. They throw in a small bottle of water, too; I am guessing it comes out of their recycled waste, but still, it's a bargain.

'I'm out of here,' I say to the angel who follows me to the cable car, preaching about the benefits of a simple life and the heavenly realm that awaits us all. I sit in the car and glance up at the Attic sky. Not that I'm expecting to see any realm awaiting. Just the flying bots and the small cheerful angels, so well-made that it's difficult to tell that they're not real. They're chanting, probably in Byzantine, but I can't be sure.

'Give my regards to Archangel Gabriel,' I say as the cable car starts whooshing down towards the foot of Lycabettus. The angel flickers next to me, the Augmented Reality is losing power. Just before it's gone, my navigator looks at me peacefully and whispers in a sweet voice.

'Don't forget about the referendum, my child. The Church needs you.'

And you need the Church, a voice inside me finishes the slogan.

> 'Problems do not get solved.'
> —*First law of social engineering*

I fill the glass with the distilled Isabella grape my parents send me every New Year's Eve, straight from the mountains of Arta. I step out on the little terrace that connects to my studio apartment, and I dust the photovoltaic off with my hand. Terraces used to be full of antennas, now they're flooded with panels and wind turbines. I gaze at Athens and wonder whether it's prettier now, than when my parents abandoned it for the countryside, along with the first great exodus wave. Would I rather gaze upon a unified concrete front, or is this asymmetric landscape of rundown neighborhoods prettier? My folks never saw the demolished blocks, the ivy climbing twenty meters high turning the abandoned office buildings green, nor did they see the old streams filling up with water once more. Well, not water exactly, this brown muddy liquid that usually flows at this time of the year. If only I didn't have to climb six flights of stairs in order to gaze upon nature attacking the city, I would probably enjoy the view more. On the other hand, if the tenants paid building fees, I wouldn't be able to afford this studio. There are plenty of empty apartments, but all the good penthouses have gone to those with fat wallets. I'm certain that their elevator works just fine, their taps run with drinking water and their electrical appliances draw power from the central network. Elevator, electricity, water. That's the failure sequence of any building's micro-society.

I go back to my room, and start munching on a bar of recycled carbohydrates. It's like eating paper. My phone rings. I answer. A man I've never seen before appears in my line of vision. He wants an appointment; I try to get a feel for the job's scale, for its objective. He vaguely explains. I agree. I go back out to the terrace. I gaze upon the city in awe, and think of its citizens unsuspectingly walking the street. They're the objective. I look towards the horizon. I try to discern the river in front of the Panathenaic Stadium, and fail.

'What's there?' I ask my navigator, an urchin missing half his leg. In the past month, my area's AR has been taken on by a non-governmental organisation that deals with vulnerable social groups, and they change the navigator every now and then. Yesterday I was guided by a homeless man, and two days ago it was a second-generation refugee.

'Nothing.'

'What do you mean, nothing? Isn't there a river over there?'

'Nothing worth mentioning.'

That's what happens when ARs come out of volunteers.

'What are the polls on the referendum?' I ask him.

'The Church is ahead, followed by the Army.'

'God help us,' I mumble and unconsciously stand at attention.

'Your problems are usually caused by
someone else's attempt at solving their own.'

The espresso sucks, it's barely drinkable. The coffeeman's only
hope would be to shove an AR chip in our taste nerve, or the
shop will go bust. The guy who made the appointment is coming
up, at least that's what the owl on my shoulder tells me.

Ἰδοῦ ὁ σὸς πέλας. Εἷσι.[1]

Some genius programmer had thought that, since he was
getting paid by lovers of the ancient Greek civilization, it would
be a brilliant idea to have the owl speak in Attic Greek, or
whatever this dialect I'm hearing is. At least he didn't give a tunic
to every passerby. My client is wearing loose Bermuda shorts,
a checkered shirt and strap sandals, as if he is ready to visit the
temple that towers above us. I haven't been up there in a long
time. Some say that it has been entirely transferred in an English
museum and we only see the AR's recreation, but I'm certain that
it's just one of the many rumours people love to spread.

'You must be Daniel One,' he says with a smile.

'And you, Alexander Zero,' I answer.

Τὸ ἐὸν ὄνομα Ἀλέξανδρός ἐστι, ἄνευ τοῦ μηδενός,[2] clarifies my
navigator, the pun going over its head.

'Just Alexandros,' the client repeats, inadvertently translating
the owl, since he can't hear what it says to me.

'OK, Alexandros. Take a seat, let me buy you an espresso.' Not
that I can afford it, but, woe if others could tell your financial status.

Alexandros pulls a metal chair and the screech pierces the
customers' ears. He doesn't seem to realise the disturbance he has
caused as he sits down; he takes a small elliptical bot out of his
pocket. It's shiny and pitch-black. He lays it next to him, beyond
the shadow shed by the coffee shop's small tent. For a little while,
it lies still under the scorching sun—for sure, some solar panel
is greedily sucking power—, and then it unfolds, revealing four
small propellers that start to spin. It rises hesitantly, maneuvering
around tables and people, and soon it is flying some ten meters

---

1. Translator's Note: There cometh your client.
2. TN: His name is Alexander, without the zero.

above us. It's looking at us, it's obvious; a small black eye that sees around us and straight inside us. I look at it too.

'Just in case,' Alexandros says with a slight smirk. 'There's a lot on the table.'

'I'm listening,' I say.

'Do you know what our problem is?'

'The referendum on the AR's grey zones.'

'Precisely. They constitute fifty percent of Athens. We want to win.'

'So do a dozen more guilds.'

He smiles. He doesn't mean it. He bends slightly towards me. 'We prefer to be called a non-governmental organisation.'

'So do a dozen more organisations.'

'That's why we hired you.'

Typical guild representative. They've certainly gotten on a high horse since they were appointed to handle the AR. He thinks I don't know that they've fallen flat on their face when they tried the same with at least five other legitimate engineers, before they ended up with me. That I'm a desperate last resort, before they lay their weapons down and accept defeat. That he detests even talking to me in this lousy coffee shop, where he wouldn't even deign to take a piss otherwise.

'I charge a lot,' I tell him.

'We pay on delivery.'

'Half as a down payment.'

'We need proof.'

'You'll have it,' I say, totally clueless as to what exactly I'm going to do. But, what kind of a screwdriver man would I be, if I didn't make promises with no return?

'Problems cannot be hidden.'
—*Second law of social engineering*

How do you convince three million people to vote for what you want? Here is a PhD thesis for social engineers, one I have to write in just a few days. If I want the money, that is. I still owe the last installment, and if I miss another one I might as well end up growing dogwood and vines up on the mountains of Arta. All right, the loan was worth it, I paid for my education on social engineering, I learned a trade. Of course, it was not enough to get a degree and register in the Chamber, but it was enough to make do on the margins of legality. The other loan, the one for the chips, is paid by my folks, no matter that they were faulty. If the Isabella tsipouro goes out of fashion, it will land on my shoulders too.

I slip into a white cotton t-shirt and go down the six floors quickly. I begin my walk. I know the basics. We have two implanted chips, one on the optic and the other on the auricular nerve; this is where the companies upload their data. I think of myself at the election venue walking towards the voting screen, looking at the ballots, wavering. How am I going to choose? What are the criteria? Motives do not vary that much. They boil down to vested interest, whatever that might mean.

Near Ampelokipoi, a wooden gavel without a hilt briefly interrupts my trail of thought. It keeps warning me of how close I am to breaking the law, since I keep ignoring the traffic lights. I am curious whether the guild that asked for my contribution are the Magistrates, but I doubt it. Even if the whole of Athens turns to ash, they would remain clueless. At most, they would declare the burning of the city as unconstitutional, and wait for the cinders to grow back into buildings.

I think of my clients. Non-governmental organisations. So they will be incorruptible, instead of ending up like the TV channels with the big time publishers. Even the stones had laughed at that argument. The point is they handle the entirety of the ads on the AR, which, to my understanding, is not exactly peanuts. That's why they sued pretty much everyone over the parts of Athens that belong to no one, but which everyone wants for their own. Now that the politicians dropped the issue like a hot potato and loaded it to the people, the guilds have the chance to break the bank. Only, they don't know on which number to place their bets. They're expecting me to tell them.

A thundering heart appears out of the corner of my eye. Not the whole heart, it misses a piece, as if some dog bit it off. That's what you get when you walk near hospitals. Good thing it's not guts. A bunch of numbers scroll in front of my eyes. Cholesterol, blood sugar, white blood cells, platelets, and a boatload of indexes—I will be damned if I have a bloody clue what they mean. Right above the passers-by, small happy syringes display epidemiological statistics, while the background crawls with trailer ads for pathologists, dermatologists, endocrinologists and psychiatrists. Loads of psychiatrists. Reasonably thinking, the Doctors don't stand a chance in the referendum, but if people made decisions based on reason I would be just another of the city's unemployed.

I return home at night, and pour some tsipouro. I let the strawberry aftertaste cool the roof of my mouth, and then I log in the screwdriver men forum. They're all cursing the politicians and the referendum. No one admits it, but the guilds have definitively recruited them for the same reason they approached me. Their curses are imaginative. Their arguments, not so much. They all come down to one line: Everyone is an asshole, except us. The guilds because they want to flood the city with their navigators, the politicians because they grab anything they can, the citizens of Athens because they will cast their ballots like sheep choosing which wolf is best to gobble them down. Reasonably, they haven't managed anything so far. They are still at point zero. Just like me.

> 'If society was a quiet stream, then social engineers would be able to steer it where they wished. However, society is a huge, impetuous river, and the only thing the engineers can do is loosen up the pressure valves, without ever knowing what is going to pop out.'

I meet Alexandros at the same coffee shop, just to spite him. I try to explain why it takes so long, that things are not as he thinks they are. I talk about multi-parametrical problems and dependent variables. He looks at me like an Eskimo first hearing of Sahara.

'I want to know who you are,' I say to him.

'That's not possible. Safety reasons. You will never know who's paying you,' Alexandros says.

Church, Army, Doctors, Educators, Shipowners, Unions and five or six more potential clients. Those who have an AR license, and some others who would love to get one. And I will never know who I'm working for.

'Then, I will need the down payment,' I say.

'Down payment comes only with proof.'

'Ten percent.'

'Deal, but you will refund it if you don't deliver the product.'

At least something came out of the appointment.

'Obviously. I will let you know as soon as I have news,' I say to him.

He smiles, all fake, as if he wanted to give away ten percent, but he frowns right after and turns to his right shoulder.

'Shut up, you turkey,' he says.

'It's an owl,' I say.

'Γλαῦξ,'[3] my navigator corrects me.

'Same thing,' Alexandros says. 'It's driving me crazy with this fucking ancient Greek since I set foot here.'

'We're under the Acropolis. What did you expect it to speak? Swahili?'

'It calls the bot 'πετόμενο μελανό λίθο'[4].'

I look at the bot above us. The navigator is not exactly wrong. Alexandros gets up and leaves quickly, continuously jerking his shoulder. The place doesn't agree with him. Perhaps he lives in the northern suburbs and the scorching downtown sun bothers him. I watch him walking away. My owl lectures me on the Parthenon Metopes, since it seized the opportunity to project a trailer of the museum's exhibits. For the first time, I realise that it is missing an eye. A black hole sits on its place, a dark window to the underworld.

'Ὁρᾷς τὴν Περσεφόνην;'[5] the navigator asks me as the eastern pediment of the Parthenon flies over the horizon.

---

3. TN: Owl.
4. TN: Flying black stone.
5. TN: Beholdest thou Persephone?

'They all look the same to me,' I say and look at the river in front of Kallimarmaro Stadium.

It's filled with a thick black liquid. A rotten boat appears in the background. The rower's black clad figure makes my skin crawl, and I unwittingly search my pockets for a coin. Fortunately, or unfortunately, they are empty.

> 'Problems accumulate.'
> —*Third law of social engineering*

Another walk around Athens. I'm running away from the National Technical University where I made the huge mistake of saying out loud, *what a cool breeze*, and a compass started chasing me in order to explain the differential equations of wind flow. As I approach the Pentagon, a ranger in camo informs me that I am in the safe location of the military operations centre. My line of vision fills with information on the potential escape routes, skirmisher positions and assembly points. Here, they're expecting a Turkish invasion, a jihadist assault or at least some severe terrorist attack any time now. Instructions of debatable value on how to feed on bitter orange skins and get water out of my distilled urine constantly crawl before me. I might need them in the future, if I find myself in the long list of the unemployed.

I go down to the subway with the navigator sharply commenting on my shave. Luckily, it fades out when the train starts; he was so grating, a few more minutes and he would call me out for the morning report. Ethniki Amyna, Katechaki, Panormou, Ampelokipoi, Megaro Mousikis, Evangelismos, Syntagma. The navigators change according to each guild's zone of influence. Stormtrooper, Einstein, Domazos, Gavel, Violin, Heart, Prostitute. What the hell! Probably some pirate AR infiltrated the network. It's almost as weird as the zone the artists managed to buy, with the help of their sponsors, filled with melting clocks and truncated figures. For a few seconds, I gawp at the half-naked chick trying to sell me addresses for wild sex. Then it blurs, becoming a hybrid of navigators and fading out to give its place to reality. All data vanish and now it's just the coach with the people inside. I'm not shocked, it's happened to me before. My AR circuit's at fault. It short-circuits when it receives powerful, competitive signals. I get out of the coach, and go up at the square. I stay still for a while. The chip restarted, but that's not important. I just found out what I'm selling to my client. It's a crazy idea, but if it works they'll all be left speechless. I never liked all these ARs anyway. Maybe it's my faulty chip, maybe it's that once or twice a year I see the world as it is, or maybe Alexandros has just pissed me off. How do you convince three million people to do what you want? You can't. But you can convince one. And sometimes, this is enough.

> 'People call social engineers screwdriver men, based on three assumptions: That society has screws, that the screwdriver men know where they are, and that they turn them in the right direction.'

The guy sitting next to me gapes and stares through the camera at the voter studying the ballots, and choosing theirs. It's the twentieth time he sees it, but he doesn't seem sated.

'Here dawns a better day,' he says.

'For all of us,' I answer.

'You're young, you weren't around during the golden age of the AR.'

'Golden for you,' I say but he probably didn't hear me. He is ecstatic at the sight of the volunteers unknowingly voting for his guild.

'Back when you could broadcast wherever and as much as you wanted. You grew up with the Independent Authority, the broadcast licenses and the influence zones.'

What should I tell him now? That I've experienced the golden age? That it was then when I got the implant, at the maternity clinic? That my optic chip broke down because three different providers happened to have a conflict in the area I was born and maxed out the power? That I see navigators with their body parts hacked off and even less data? Better not, because he might realise how I got the idea that solves his problem.

'So, heightening the intensity would be enough?'

'Take it up to eleven. If your AR prevails, if the voters only see your navigator, you have the referendum in your pocket.'

In fact, I don't have to say anything. The thirtieth voter is already on his way to the ballot screen, and twenty-eight of them have chosen what my client wants.

'I knew you would make it,' he says.

He didn't have a clue. I was the one-in-the-million chance that played out, or at least that's what he thinks.

'Really? How come?'

'You're a social engineer. Your job is to sway society to do whatever you want.'

He's so mistaken that I almost pity him. Almost.

'Right. I'm waiting for the down payment,' I say.

A more humble client might be a bit more reticent. He would say that it's a small scale simulation, that in vitro is different from in vivo, that we should wait for the real referendum. A more humble person.

'You'll get it,' he says, excited.

'What are you going to do about the Authority? It might hinder the signal boost,' I say.

'Don't worry. We have our ways.'

Before I go, he whispers to me, in fake confidence: 'I admit that at the beginning, I thought that a social engineer is an asshole who's going to solve our problem.'

'That's OK. Screwdriver men know that only half of that is true.'

He laughs and extends his hand towards me. I look at it, smile and leave.

At night, I log in the screwdriver men forum again. They're in a frenzy, but it seems that they're still all groping in the dark. They don't have faulty chips to inspire them. If I let slip a word, I'll let them all in on the trick. Just a word.

'It is noteworthy that the less well-known law
of social engineering is the fundamental one.'

The day of the referendum, I walk to the Acropolis and go up
to the Parthenon. There is no ticket booth, today everything is
free, people should vote while pleased. I stand on the edge of the
hill, Athens splayed on my feet. It's still early, but the show will
start in a bit and I don't want to miss out on the spectacle. The
one-eyed owl gazes at the landscape too. The buzzing of a flying
black rock makes me turn. Here comes Just Alexandros.

'I didn't think I would find you here,' he says.

'Neither did I.'

'I came to enjoy the spectacle.'

'It'll be one to remember,' I say, but he doesn't realize a thing.
He smiles and walks away pleased.

The city looks so beautiful. The Acropolis AR changes its
display in the blink of an eye, now projecting Ancient Athens.
A dreamy landscape with streams, grass, small temples and the
crowded agora. It almost makes you believe it could be like that
again. A city of a few thousand residents, living off agriculture
and livestock. But, gradually, things change. The owl starts to
transform, it keeps the wings, but it becomes whiter, brighter.
An angel takes its place. The ancient temples fade out, replaced
by small chapels and chants. The Church started boosting their
signal. Very soon, the other guilds catch up. They must have
gotten the intel form the other screwdriver men in the forums.
The chapels become citadels and then football fields. Out of the
corner of my eye, I see Alexandros gesturing constantly, talking
to someone invisible. I smile. It started and apparently, it's going
fine.

Within a few minutes everything has blurred into a huge
muddle, into an AR mash-up, as good as the best surrealist
painting. Maradona is wearing night goggles and speaks ancient
Greek with a perfect accent. The one-eyed owl is issuing court
orders with a paint brush in hand. Picasso scores one goal after
another in a surgeon's scrubs, while the crowd's cheering for him.
Jesus Christ is getting ready to join the army, but the supervisor

urges him to have a haircut first. I imagine the antennae operators constantly boosting up the signal, raising the intensity to the maximum. Athenians must have gone nuts. They must be watching angels fighting with owls and listening to military orders in ancient Attic dialect. My head feels as if it's about to explode, pretty much as I might have felt the day my chip broke down. For a moment, everything goes black. I don't see or hear anything. Peace.

Then, the real Athens unfolds before me. It's not as ugly as I thought it would be. Without the AR goodies it just seems poorer, but way more real. Like a king robbed off his fancy clothes, only to be left as just another human being. If everything went well, the rest of the city residents must be looking at the same sight. Alexandros has sat down and holds his head between his hands. His chip must have short-circuited too. What are we going to do now, without the ARs? They were a solution, though us, screwdriver-men, all know that there are no solutions. Just problems.

Before I go, I look at the river in front of the Kallimarmaro stadium. I smile, bitterly. It's not even a river. It's totally empty, a huge drain filled with garbage and rubble. Some big-ass-mayor must have had it dug just to impress and then abandoned it. A scar in the heart of Athens to remind us of our past glory. What it will become of it? Maybe my fellow citizens will wake up. Now that they have no AR to fool them, they might make something useful out of this small urban gorge. If you're asking me though, I believe they will fuck it up again. They will turn it into a dump, they will fill it with rubble, or at best, they will cover it up and fill it with the city's sewage waste. I wish they proved me wrong.

I start on my way back. I wonder what I'll do next. I got rid of the chip loan, but I guess I won't be very popular as an engineer for a few years. In fact, I won't even get the rest of the payment, though I did my job just fine. In the end, maybe the problem is that people have failed to fully understand the laws of social engineering. Memorizing them is not enough, they need to apply them as well. Things would fare much better then. But who cares what I think? I'm but an ex-screwdriver man, an ex-asshole who they thought would solve their problems.

Come to think of it, this is a good option. Ex-screwdriver man solves the problem of the currently burnout. Wrong. He doesn't solve them. He takes them on. Certainly, there must be thousands of us suffering from post-traumatic stress disorders. It's not a bad career alternative. It would be a shame to let all these psychology classes I took to become an engineer go to waste. I will tell my clients to lie down on a couch and ask them to imagine that horrendous drain as a normal river. So many ARs and none tried to fill it with clear water, to let it gargle, to place little rocking boats in it with happy children on board. That's what I'm going to tell my clients. The only AR that's worth it is your imagination. It doesn't solve any problems, but it allows you to live with them. Until the day that you'll understand the fundamental law of social engineering: *There is only one way to solve a problem. Not to create it.*

The Human(c)ity of Athens
Ioanna Bourazopoulou

Translators from Greek: Dimitra Nikolaidou, Vaya Pseftaki

Stationmaster Madebo strolled around the block, checking out the neoclassical buildings with the plaster decorations, where only high-ranking governmental officials could possibly be residing. It was almost six in the morning and the soft early light was dispelling the night's darkness. It was still early for his appointment, but since he didn't know this city, he preferred to arrive ahead so he wouldn't risk being late.

He pulled up the sleeves of his blazer and gazed at the contrast between the olive-leaf colored fabric and the dark complexion of his wrist. In Lubumbashi, the Stationmaster's uniform was cobalt blue, too dark for his skin, while this warm shade was very pleasing to the eye, accenting the smoothness of his ebony complexion. Could this be an upgrade?

For the hundredth time, he checked the digital map in his watch. The bright blinking dot was him, he was definitely at the right spot. He clicked on the sound icon to hear how this street was pronounced. *Διονυσίου Αρεοπαγίτου*, the digital voice informed him. He slowed down the voice speed setting to hear it again, to capture the intonation of the consonants. The digital voice uttered the syllables of the street name again. He brought the watch to his lips and tried to pronounce it himself, 'Dionysiou Areopagitou.' A red graph flashed on the screen, indicating the syllables where the pronunciation was off. Despite last week's crash course in Greek, his accent remained French. Athens' official languages blinked on the margins of the screen: English, German, Greek. He wondered in which of them he should greet the Commissioner, when he felt a light tapping on his shoulder.

'Good morning! Gutten Morgen! Καλημέρα, Stationmaster Madebo!' came a female voice.

Surprised, he turned around, took off his kepi and reciprocated in English. Commissioner Axiothea looked a lot like her photograph, so he didn't have a hard time recognizing her, despite the fact that she wasn't wearing her uniform today. She was a petite and incredibly dexterous woman, wearing her white hair in a sleek bob cut, with elfin Asian features and sparkling black eyes. She was wearing a blue tracksuit and trainers that made her look like a teenager with a sixty-year-old's head. She must have started jogging early on; her cheeks were flushed and she didn't look as she was about to stop. She circled him in a light jog, forcing him to revolve around himself in order to maintain eye contact.

'"Διονυσίου Αρεοπαγίτου"', Stationmaster Madebo,' she corrected him, as she had obviously heard him practicing. 'Your 'r' is too melodic, or your watch's language software needs upgrading.'

'I promise I'll try harder,' he answered, mindful of his 'r'.

'Sehr gut, Bahnhofsvorsteher!' The Commissioner could not hide her surprise for the instant improvement of his pronunciation. 'You're a very quick learner. You will soon be speaking English, German and Greek as fluently as an Athenian.'

She signaled for him to follow her and resumed jogging along the uphill road. Stationmaster Madebo hesitated for a moment, but shortly he tucked his kepi under his arm and started running behind her. He caught up and tried to fall in step with her so that they could jog at the same pace. The soles of his shoes weren't soft, like hers, and they hit the paved street noisily, embarrassing him.

'I suggest that we continue our talk in Greek,' said the Commissioner, keeping her panting impressively under control. 'Since you have worked in Delhi and Johannesburg, I'm confident that your English and German is sufficient.'

'Es ist wahr, at least I suppose so,' he confirmed.

'French-accented, though,' she smiled. 'Is this your first visit in Europe?'

'Yes, I arrived yesterday, at midnight. Today is my first day in the city,'

'And, in less than forty minutes from now, you will have to support its best interests.' She stopped running and stood breathless by the side of the paved street. The sunrays peeked golden through the columns of the Acropolis and shed light on the stone steps of the Herod Atticus Odeon. On the banks of the road, street vendors started to appear, like caterpillars in array. They set up small stalls and arranged their merchandise. Madebo had the impression that they were all selling exactly the same things.

'I am aware that a week of training is not enough to prepare you for your new position,' the Commissioner said. 'You will have to welcome the new Athenians, as a host, when you yourself have only been an Athenian for a few hours. Unfortunately, time is a luxury we sacrificed for the sake of development. You are familiar with a Stationmaster's duties, as well as with the importance we place on the welcoming ceremony, so I am certain that you know what is expected from you.'

'Of course.' Madebo smiled, revealing his perfect teeth, with their blinding whiteness highlighting the beauty of his ebony face. 'I am well aware of how defining first impressions are for the new citizens. I've welcomed the new citizens of Lubumbashi for five years.'

'If I may, Lubumbashi's Station is very different from Athens' Station,' she interrupted him. 'Lubumbashi is the capital of mines. Its power is lying beneath the ground and the citizens must learn to love a treasure hidden out of sight—not just love it, but adore it—as this is the only way they will passionately seek to extract it from the belly of the earth and bring it to the surface. This means that when you greet them, even your body language, the tone of your voice, the way you incline your head or move your hands, everything must reflect and evoke this unbridled desire for mining. Right from the start, you have to draw their interest towards the underground so that they will be distracted by the natural beauty of the landscape and seek instead the mystery of the underground tunnels, the coolness of the half-dark labyrinths, the glow of the buried metals. You put it quite correctly before: first impressions are defining, especially when the preparation time becomes more and more limited, the citizens reach their new city without having the opportunity to come to terms with the idea of relocation. In short, we are expecting of you to use your skills in order to cover for the time we didn't give them.'

'I understand completely,' he confirmed. He wished he himself wouldn't manifest any lack of adaptability symptoms, or at least that they wouldn't be visible.

Axiothea eyed him quite satisfied. Madebo justified the choice of those who deemed him suitable for this position. Tall, upright, ebony, with his immaculate uniform and polished wingtip shoes, he could hardly go unnoticed. She saw street vendors casting curious and admiring glances towards him.

'You have an imposing figure and a cultured voice, an impressive talent for languages and, what's more, your uniform suits you; all these are important qualifications for a reception Stationmaster.' The Commissioner walked through the stalls, inspecting their merchandise at the same time. 'The first bullet train of the day arrives at half past six sharp. The people you are about to welcome received their relocation order a few days or a few hours ago. For some of them, it's the first time in Europe, for some it's their first time in the Balkans, some can't even find Athens on a map and they had never even fathomed that they would be registered in this city's workforce. They feel unprepared and confused, not knowing whether this relocation is a punishment or a reward, a demotion or a promotion. The train car doors will open and the first thing they'll see will be the pier, the first authority figure they will recognize will be you, the first voice they'll hear will be yours. For the next three minutes you will have their absolute attention, and in these three minutes you will have to convey to them, with clarity and persuasiveness, the essence of their new city and of their new mission. Research has shown that they never forget the moment of their arrival; your words will forever remain etched in their mind, every nod, every movement, every expression on your face.'

The street vendors watched them in silence, without even attempting to get close to them or catch their attention. The Commissioner in the tracksuit, with her Asian features, wasn't a stranger. They concluded that the dark skinned man who accompanied her didn't belong to the city's new workforce either, so there was no point in trying to sell him their fares. The stalls were targeting the passengers of the first train that would arrive at half past six sharp.

'So, come on Stationmaster, talk to me about Athens. Convince me that you have formed an accurate interpretation of the city and that you are able to convey it.' Axiothea set the timer on her watch and the seconds marched on.

Madebo cleared his throat and started reciting. 'Citizens of Athens, welcome to the city of the god Hermes. A city which through your hard work and dedication-'

'No, no,' the Commissioner interrupted, 'I don't want the Stationmaster's Welcoming Speech, I am certain that you've rehearsed it plenty of times in front of the mirror. I want you to convey your own perception of Athens, now that you're walking through its historical centre.'

The historical centre? This district was so different from the rest, those he had to cross to get here, so full of skyscrapers and shopping centers that it looked like an anachronistic joke. Beautiful mansions, marble columns, hills covered with ancient monuments, trenches filled with the ruins of the Ancient Agora. His view of the city? He hadn't had time to form one and neither had he intended to, knowing that it would prove totally useless. The only thing he cared about was to speed up the adaptability procedure, to erase Lubumbashi from his mind, the sweet warmth of the afternoon, the house with the palm trees, the image of Emma waving at him from the kitchen window, moving little Sebastian's hand too while he was half-asleep in her arms.

He turned towards the East and, hoping that he was pointing at the right spot, he said: 'Over there, in the background, is the

Pnyx hill, where Athenians used to gather for their democratic assembly, a… uhm… political body. The idea of democracy was born on these hills…'

'The illusion of democracy,' Axiothea corrected him. 'It's important to be accurate when you express your personal view, or else your discomfiture might be perceived as admiration. History is being re-examined under the light of the admissions of the International Development Plan; Greek antiquity was nothing but an era of deliberate beguilement. The idea of the city weighed so heavy that it crushed the citizens who fought for the city and not for themselves, who struggled to be worthy of it, and boasted because they originated from it, as if where you come from could ever equilibrate a trivial life, and they looked down on anyone who didn't have ancestral tombs on its grounds. The city's dictatorship, a crime that started on these hills and lasted for millennia, camouflaged as an ideal, annihilating more personalities and lives than all wars combined. It was not until our own era of sobriety, the era of humanistic economy, that humans were delivered from the shackles of the city.'

It is certainly an upgrade, Emma said, giving him back the relocation order without reading it, and continued to feed Sebastian. Madebo didn't share her conviction; he would hold the same position, the same rank, the exact same duties. Yes, but in another city and in another uniform, it is an upgrade, she briskly decided. They stood silent, looking at Sebastian toying with his food, while they tried to come to terms with the idea of separation, to convince themselves that breaking their common course, losing the words, the gazes, the warmth of their bodies at night was worth it. Emma took Sebastian in her arms, when are you leaving? In a week.

'We separated the fate of humanity from the fate of the city,' the Commissioner stressed, 'this was the achievement of the humanistic economy. The International Development Plan was based on very simple admissions. What is the city? A steady developmental convention, defined by invariable characteristics, such as its geographic location, its mineral wealth, its morphology, its climate. What is the human? A dynamic developmental convention, defined by variable characteristics, such as skills, abilities, performance. There is no reason for these two poles of development to co-exist, unless they benefit mutually. Citizens who develop incompatible characteristics are relocated in cities where these characteristics will manifest in a beneficial way and will be harnessed efficiently. We are careful to match the potential of each city with each citizen's skills, as it's the only way to generate civilization!'

If only we had a second child, Emma brought her fingers to his lips to silence him—she was trying to put the boy to sleep. Valdes, who has three children, relocated together with his wife, he whispered to her. He is a financial analyst, Emma reminded him, it's not the same. Then it'd be better if we didn't have any children at all, Madebo thought bitterly. If it wasn't for Sebastian you wouldn't have to stay up all night, you'd be focused and well-rested, you'd perform better and you could be upgraded too. They would never send me to Athens, Emma said, reading his mind, I'm a chemist, they need me in the mines. I need you too, Emma.

'Living in a city that doesn't provide the right work opportunities and challenges leads to neuroses, depression and suicidal tendencies, not to mention the destructive consequences on productivity,' the Commissioner said shaking her head disapprovingly. 'On top of that, it is responsible for the foulest forms of collectivity. Simple admissions: heterogeneous groups are unstable and self-destructive because, eventually, their members will prey on each other in an agonizing attempt to eliminate their differences. Then collectivity turns into a tragedy and citizens resort to isolation to protect themselves from the unnatural grouping. The reason contemporary Humancities guarantee safety and peace is because they host homogeneous workforce; there are no rusty traditions, no personal relationships tarnished by time, no ancestral imperatives and responsibilities, no tyrannical superstitions bound to soil and blood. The city is always preserved like new, and so are its citizens.'

We are eternal immigrants, Emma whispered, how could we think that Lubumbashi would last forever? Madebo held her tight in his arms and rested his head on the pillow. The bluish light from his son's room entered through the half-closed bedroom door, making Emma's pale complexion glow like the moon. She came from Reykjavik, five years after Winnipeg, three years after Aachen; he came from Johannesburg, six years after Delhi, four years after Ibadan. They'd been travelling for hours in the same carriage and they finally introduced themselves to each other in Lubumbashi's Welcoming Station, when they almost mixed up their luggage. They stepped on their new city at the same time, same pace and same gaze, and maybe that was why Lubumbashi was the only corner of the Earth where he didn't feel a stranger; because her body, wrapped around his at night, was his only homeland.

'The modern citizen is a complex personality, Stationmaster Madebo, he can't always keep control of his desires and priorities,' Axiothea explained. 'He's often overpowered by obsessions, urges and immature emotions, consequently preventing his own development, pursuing social delay, without realizing that he is propelling himself into absolute misery. The International Development Plan's mechanisms intervene correctively, guiding him, training him, relocating him, incessantly assessing him, so that his creativity isn't reduced. Our natural goal is self-realisation, and self-realisation is achieved only through efficient work. Same goes for the city, its natural goal is development, continuous and unhindered development; we keep the cities prosperous by constantly renewing their workforce.'

The preparation days were hell, the thought that he wouldn't see them again, that Emma and Sebastian would go on with their lives without him, it made him desperate. He considered applying for co-service by exception, but he didn't know who to address. Lubumbashi answered to Kinshasa, Kinshasa to Ontario, Ontario to Tokyo, Tokyo to New York, New York to Paris, Paris to Sao Paolo, a chain of interlinked centers, where it was impossible to locate the starting or the ending point. Trains, planes and ships daily transferred new citizens to the Humancities of the world, new supervisors, judges and commissioners, none of whom liked exceptions, schedule diversions, anomalies. He tried talking to his colleagues, but they were all new, some upgraded, some downgraded, his neighbors also, his relatives' tracks lost between relocations. He felt all alone on a globe overflowing with people, a planet full of individual destinies which never crossed unless by chance or occasion.

We will get used to it in time, Emma caressed his cheek, everyone gets used to it eventually. He dreaded the truth of this statement, because when he saw the sun rising from this hemisphere of the earth, he felt as if he was gone for months from the house with the palm trees, when it had only been three days since the heartbreaking parting. He sobbed on the train to Kinshasa, he boarded the plane to Cairo sullen and he slept on the ferry to Piraeus, exhausted. He was calm when he reached the port and caught the train to Thiseion. Only then did he realize that the next day he would be the one to welcome the passengers of this route and he studied the faces of the travelers in his carriage with a professional interest, as well as his reflection on the window glass. He got off the train at Thiseion Station and listened carefully to the Stationmaster's welcoming, feeling anticipation mixed with anguish and the deep, familiar, imposing feeling of inevitability. He admired the majestic figure of his predecessor up on the gallery and wondered whether he himself would manage so well, whether the uniform in the colour of the olive leaf would suit him.

'Humanistic economy brought humans closer to their real nature and cities closer to their real destiny.' They were going down Apostolou Pavlou street and the Thiseion Station's arches were visible by the end of the pedestrian walkway. 'Athens spent many centuries in obscurity, under the illusion that it is the city of philosophers and viticulturists, until it came to terms with its real potential for development. Simple admissions: Athens soil is neither rich nor farmable; the land is rocky and arid, poor in flora and fauna, so it falls short on almost every field of productivity. The only aces up its sleeve are its location on the world map, right on the crossroad where three continents meet, its Attic light and mild climate, which encourage a pleasant disposition and benefit communication. In short, it offers an ideal environment for commercial affairs! It's the capital of commerce, that's why its citizens turned to the sea right away, to the exploration of the waterways, to the development of language and the logic of numbers, to the establishment of alliances. God Hermes is its protector, not goddess Athena,' she picked a Hermes statuette and showed it to him, 'it's heart beats in the Ancient Agora, exactly where we stand right now, not where you showed me earlier, in Pnyx. The Athenians' gifts are excellent means of expression and negotiation skills, not contemplation and strategic thought, as it was falsely claimed in the past. Based on these criteria, we now renew its workforce, in order to help the city play the part the International Development Plan has chosen on its behalf. The new Athenians you are about to welcome have to make this vision come true. Their initiation will start with your welcoming, and shall continue with the experience of commercial affairs offered to them by these trained commissioners of god Hermes, which you can see around you,' she pointed to the street vendors. 'We are aware of how defining first impressions are, and that's why we have carefully planned their first walk into the city. They will have to cross the pedestrian street of Apostolou Pavlou and Dionysiou Areopagitou in order to get to the means of transport located by the Columns of the Olympian Zeus. A fifteen minute walk they will never forget, as the professionals you see around you are very well aware of the emotion they must convey. When they arrive at the Columns of the Olympian Zeus, they will have felt to their very bones that the soul and the culture of the Humancity of Athens is the art of trade. So, are you able to kickstart them on their educational experience?'

'I will do my best,' Madebo said.

'I am certain. What's left is to wish you good luck,' Axiothea said and shook his hand. 'I'm looking forward to reading the evaluation report your Director will send me.' She pulled up the hood of her tracksuit and took off in a light jog.

Madebo secured the kepi on his head and quickly went down the marble stairs of the Welcoming Station, as if he'd been going up and down these stairs all his life. He crossed the underground corridor and reached the staff entrance—luckily, all Reception

Stations had the exact same layout. He pulled up his sleeve, touched his naked wrist on the door screen and allowed the digital inspector to verify his identity. The blue ray read the implanted code and the door opened with a soft buzz. The moment he passed through the entrance, Lubumbashi had been forever erased from his memory.

The security guards greeted him with respect, skillfully hiding their surprise. Most of them hadn't been informed about this change, but relocations were so frequent that they had already been reconciled with the image of their new supervisor even before Madebo replied to their greeting.

He checked the power and ventilation indexes, unlocked the gate that lead to the gallery of the pier—he would ask to put the handle on the other side, since he was left-handed—, and stood at the centre of the gallery, tall, hegemonic, imposing like a statue. The time was twenty nine past six. He opened the metallic drawer, took the wireless microphone device that resembled a brooch and pinned it on the collar of his uniform. He pronounced his name and his voice echoed all over the place; the sound reproduction was perfect. He made sure that the security guards had taken their places along the pier and gestured towards the control to secure the exits the moment the R1 train, loaded with new Athenians, arrived silently into the station.

The doors opened and the passengers came out of the carriages pulling their wheeled suitcases behind them. Madebo didn't recognize himself in their startled, worried faces any more. Standing on the marble gallery, visible from everywhere on the pier, almighty, he waited until all eyes were on him.

'Citizens of Athens, welcome to the city of the god Hermes.'

His deep voice echoed imposing and confident, restoring their faith in the future within their troubled souls. He slowly repeated each phrase in all three languages, Greek, English and German. He explained how they would benefit themselves and the humanistic economy as well, if they engaged in commercial development with consistency and dedication, if they facilitated the course of both products and services from the supplier to the buyer, from the producer to the consumer, from one continent to the other. They will now orderly proceed to the digital inspectors, where their identity will be verified and after that, the employees will provide them with their new professional card and the keys to their new apartment. They have reached their true destination, they are now masters of their destiny and they will fulfill all their dreams, if only they never forget…

'…πως μόνο η δουλειά ελευθερώνει! Work sets you free! Arbeit macht frei!'

Baghdad Square
Michalis Manolios

Translators from Greek: Dimitra Nikolaidou, Vaya Pseftaki

'What is this huge arc in Pedion Areos Park?'

I noticed the inconsistency when we had already been together with Dragomir for three years, but of course, at that point I didn't recognize it as such. I was getting dressed in the twenty-first floor of the Athens Tower, Alexandra's Avenue spreading beneath my feet, a river of red and white lights extending from Kifisias to Patision Avenue. I was putting on his shirt without hurrying. I liked my dates with Dragomir because they emitted this sense of effortless reality—this and the awesome sex, that is. And he himself was a very careful man, with a meticulous love of verisimilitude. Except for the office with the impressive view that had been turned into a hotel room, everything else was, and was supposed to unfold, as in real life: we came and went on foot, we had to undress and dress, I was not overstimulated, he didn't possess unnatural stamina. Even our bodies were normal, not stunning, their flaws obvious; I had copied my actual body and I believed him that he had done the same.

'All right, I know you don't give a damn about current affairs, but not even that?' He was still lying down, his arms behind his head and that satisfied smile on his lips. He enjoyed, he had said, watching me getting dressed. I don't know what he got from that, I always wore shapeless work clothes or camo, but I was even worse at undressing, so I took it as an unexpected compliment.

I shrugged and turned to him. 'Drago, how would you like it

if we met?'

His smile went away.

'Don't worry, I don't want us to change all that,' I said pointing around me. 'Nor do I intend to be a clinger on the outside. I'm having a great time here, and I'd like it if we'd met. Just to get a cup of coffee, that's all.'

He noticed then. 'You've put on my shirt,' he said, and the smile returned.

I looked at my hands buttoning it up, as if I had made a mistake in the half-light.

'Go on,' he said and I knew I would see him in real life.

*

Well, I did not see him, and this saddened me much, but for the wrong reasons. We fit unexpectedly well with Dragomir. A married father of two, he only wanted some harmless fun. He loved his family and only had good things to say for his wife. I liked that, I was even a bit envious. I was also married and had a child, but my own choices in life were less successful. We didn't leave the room, but we talked a lot when we weren't having any other kind of fun, and we ordered food and drinks once in a while. It was the week's feast for both of us.

The virtuality helped, of course. You were supposedly getting a midday nap, and no harm was done. The systems were now superfast, speeding time up to eight times, everything was internal, no cables and no external equipment, all done through Embodied Computers. No health or pregnancy risks, you were completely safe without leaving your house even for a moment and, every bit as important, your body could not tell virtual from real joy.

Which is why I found it strange when he set our appointment at Phylis street. He said there were some nice coffee shops there, but I only knew of the brothels. On the other hand, the times when I ran around the city were long gone, and current affairs were not my forte, indeed, so it wasn't unlikely that some important change in the city centre's character had passed me by—like the monstrous arc that I had spotted in Pedion Areos during our last date. Yet the arc wasn't there, which took me by surprise. If it was any other man I wouldn't even have spotted it—you do not expect virtualities to faithfully copy reality, on the contrary—but Dragomir was renting us an Athens tourist package, so such inconsistencies were out of the question. I scratched my head and made a mental note to ask about that, and continued towards Phylis street and the nice coffee shops.

Fuck coffee shops. The brothels, they were there. Red lights, or yellow, or none at all. Basements, or a couple of steps below sad doors. Disdain was also there, on the faces of young men going door to door, on this Friday night at nine o' clock. Greeks, Bulgarians, Romanians, Russians, Georgians, Pakistani, Syrians, Iraqi; only a Native American was missing. Most were between twenty and thirty, some almost forty, a few were even older. Damn you, Drago, the last thing a woman wants is to stand alone in a corner among such a horny, patchwork pack.

He had not set the date in a coffee shop, he had said we will meet at the corner of Phylis and Feron, we will walk together and you can pick up the place. Whatever you say. I lowered my head; it was the first time he was letting me down. The gazes of the men around me were disgusting. Not to the point of being crude, nobody said anything. It was just that the place stripped their thoughts bare. *Are you for sale?* My clothes dropped no such hint, khaki pants and a jacket zipped up to the chin, but the hormones didn't stop burning behind their eyes.

For safety reasons, we hadn't exchanged phone numbers. I logged in the forum where I had met him and left him an angry message, that he had stood me up and he should hurry the fuck up and take me away from there. I gave him five more minutes, during which I turned my gaze around so the cameras of my Embodied Computer could pick up everything, and then I disappeared. There would be hell to pay.

*

But there wasn't.

'You do understand you are not getting any tonight, right?' I asked, arms crossed on my chest.

'Where were you? I waited for you for more than half an hour.'

'Drago, we promised, no lies between us. I've been at the corner of Phylis and Feron since five to nine. If you had bothered to come, you could easily spot me between the hordes of horny men getting in and out of the brothels.'

He jerked his head back in surprise. 'I did bother to come,' he said, offended. 'But there are no brothels in Phylis. And yes, we promised no lies, and that goes for both of us.'

'There are no brothels in Phylis,' I repeated just in case I believed it.

'Look,' he said and raised his hands in a reconciliatory manner, 'we're obviously dealing with a matter of trust. I can take you to the coffee shops at Phylis *now*. You know we are in a faithful, dynamic…'

'…in a faithful, dynamic copy of Athens. I know.' I turned to the window with the impressive view. It was afternoon, the virtual sun had not set yet, and the mysterious arc of dubious aesthetic was still where Pedion Areos was supposed to be. 'Yes,' I said. 'Let's go so you can show me.'

*

He didn't have to show me anything. This monstrosity was forty meters high. And it didn't stand on its own. Almost three hundred meters beyond it was an almost identical arc. I had seen them from the bus, of course, but when we got to where the statue of King Constantine the First was supposed to be, two hands sprouted out of the earth instead, crossing a pair of steel swords as long as two buses each.

'The Hands of Victory,' Dragomir said, in a tour guide tone. 'Forty-three metres long swords. The hands are a copy of Saddam's hands. One of them even has his fingerprint on the thumb.'

I picked my jaw up. If I didn't know how meticulous he was with verisimilitude, I would reject this whole circus of a spectacle as a kink of the virtuality. Yet Dragomir had rented one of the good tourist packages, one regularly updated. I knew it because I was paying half of it—and it wasn't cheap. I didn't like the fake, plastic dating environments, and he believed that the tourist ones were the most unlikely place to bump on someone you knew.

Then I noticed the people. My gaze had been stuck upwards, at the swords. When I lowered it in front of us, I noticed the virtual border and the people on both sides.

'What's going on here?' I asked, dazed.

It was Dragomir's turn to be puzzled. He looked at me suspiciously and then he began explaining, but he did so with disbelief apparent in his voice. 'If you don't know what's going on here, you've been away from Athens for too long, my fair lady, and this is not what we agreed upon when we decided to be mutually sincere.' He paused, but it seems that my confused face convinced him to go on. 'Baghdad gets to know Athens from as close as possible.'

People talked or gestured in front of an invisible line separating the two cities.

'I've never lied to you. How did they bring Baghdad here?'

Dragomir crossed his arms on his chest. He still thought that I was playing pretend and that he was forced to say things we both knew. 'They did not,' he huffed, 'it's only a projection. We can go through the border, and then you'll see the statue of King Constantine and Pedion Areos behind it. As long as we stand in front of it, you see and hear the Great Celebration Square with the Hands of Victory on both its edges.'

We got closer to the virtual border. It was clear where Athens stopped and Baghdad began, but it was hard to swallow that the people in front of me weren't there in the flesh. Bearded men, women in hijabs and shabbily dressed children walked in the background, in the big, devoid of cars avenue uniting the two arcs. Some waved from afar, but lots stood in the border and talked in English with the Greeks, or in Arabic with Iraqi immigrants.

I turned and looked at Dragomir. I must have had a little girl's gaze because the disbelief on his face cracked a bit. They were smiling. People seemed to enjoy the contact. Strangers met with strangers, men and women they would probably never see again. They said hello, exchanged well-wishes or opinions, I couldn't hear from where we stood, but it seemed like a unique experience. Most stood for a little while and then left. Others, most of them

Iraqi immigrants, seemed to have appointments with relatives or friends.

'A chance to meet for free, without travel expenses or virtuality fees,' Dragomir said. 'A hundred times more live than Skype. Come,' he added and took me by the elbow.

We approached the border at a point where there weren't too many people.

'We'll pass through…' Dragomir began, but then an Iraqi woman lifted her hand and waved at me. She was wearing a purple hijab and had a ten year old boy by her side. They were both coming towards us, probably so they could cross through the border too. A moment before they did, she simply smiled, lifted her hand and greeted me, looking me in the eye.

'Salaam.'

A woman of Baghdad had greeted me. It was one of the most wonderful things that have ever happened to me. I was left with my own hand raised and a stupid expression spread on my face, without knowing if she had seen my own greeting.

'We're going through,' Dragomir said. Half of him had already disappeared beyond the border. I would have been surprised by the spectacle, if just a moment ago I hadn't been greeted by a mother in a purple hijab, at the entrance of Pedion Areos. At Baghdad Square, I thought. I was in Baghdad Square.

In a dazed moment, I went through the border and the Arabian sounds instantly disappeared.

'Usually they prefer parks or squares as interface spots, because they offer plenty of space at the border so that people can meet.'

I saw the statue of King Constantine and turned around. The border was an almost vertical, transparent, colorless bubble. Nothing was projected on it, while behind it people seemed to look and gesture at nothing.

'Why Baghdad?' I asked.

'I don't know,' he shrugged. 'Usually, the coupling is made with cities with which we have some connection. Very often it's the Balkans, Turkey, Europe. Less often the Mediterranean, Asia and other continents. At some point we had sent soldiers to Iraq, it could be that; I am not familiar with the algorithm.'

Children played under the statue. Pedion Areos, behind it, looked just as I always knew it. I took Dragomir's hand and we strolled in front of the border again.

'You really had no idea, did you?' he asked.

'I've never lied to you about anything. OK, so maybe on our first times together, I wasn't really having orgasms. But, I truly have no idea.'

He laughed out loud. 'All right. The coupling with each city lasts from one to two weeks. Apart from the people, it's also good for commerce and entrepreneurship. Though you cannot exchange anything material, it is not unusual for professionals to meet at each border. They say it's a much better ice-breaker. Also, if we circled the border, you'd find out it reaches almost to the back, at Moustoxydi street. Very often, cultural events are organized at the periphery, many of them supported by both sides. This is why the coupling schedule is set up quite early on...'

'I would love to see something li-'

I stopped as soon as I saw the wooden, black and white kiosk. I hadn't noticed it when we first arrived; my mind was on the swords, and on the people.

'Oh, yes,' Dragomir said. 'Not everyone is happy when different peoples contact each other.'

Black t-shirts, meanders and Greek flags. They distributed pamphlets. I took one. The indisputable purity of the Greek people, the increase of illegal immigrants because of the couplings, the loss of Greek jobs, the illnesses the immigrants bring with them.

'At least they aren't shouting today,' Dragomir said and showed me the policemen drinking instant coffee on their feet a bit further down. 'Once a week they are allowed to have a bullhorn. Sometimes, some other fellows in hoods or helmets come down upon them, all wound up. It's no fun. Well, it is, but only if you are on the other side of the border with your pop-corn and your coke at hand.'

I threw the pamphlet in a rubbish bin. 'Drago, we have to figure out what's happening,' I said.

'You obviously don't know about SEF either.'

'The Peace and Friendship Stadium? What about it?'

'That's where the second coupling tends to take place. I think these days we are coupled with Berlin. Almost always, we have a city with a lower standard of living in one coupling, and another with a higher one in the other. It helps to remember how far you have come and set new goals.'

I turned to look at him.

'If none of us is lying...'

'I haven't proven to you yet that I am not lying,' he interrupted me. 'Let's go. We will go brothel crawling at Phylis.'

*

There were no brothels. Neither red lights nor yellow. Disdain wasn't there. There were Greeks, Bulgarians, Romanians, Russians, Georgians, Pakistani, Syrians, Iraqi, yet they were not a horny pack, but a peaceful patchwork. Not that I wasn't expecting it after all that, but the picture was still impressive. The whole of Phylis and the streets around it had been gentrified into something much closer to the historical centre of Athens. The meticulous aesthetics of the shops and the money that had obviously been invested in the area, in many cases had nothing to envy of Thiseio or Monastiraki. After a short stroll, with my eyebrows arching higher and higher, we ended up in a coffee shop with comfy sofas and cups of fragrant chocolate.

'Look,' I said, 'I didn't expect to actually need it, but I took a video of Phylis full of brothels, just to show you that I was there on time.'

I projected the video in front of us and watched him increasingly frown.

'This is obviously Phylis street before the gentrification. I cannot see how you could have recorded that a few days ago. Don't be surprised, but I did the same.'

It was not the first time this was happening. One of the reasons we fit so well together, was that we often reacted to things the same way. Our thoughts followed very similar paths, sometimes even identical ones. In Dragomir's video, Phylis was just as I saw it now all around me. Elegant shops, carefree people strolling around or drinking their coffee and chatting. The corner of Phylis and Feron, where I had been stood up, looked like a magic eye picture. It was so similar to what I was seeing in the tourist package, that it crossed my mind that he had taken the video in here. Only that I now noticed the sign at the coffee shop next to us.

'Look,' I said, 'the shop nearby had a different sign.'

'Yes,' he said taking his eyes off the video. 'They still haven't refreshed it in here. Such small changes take a few days, I imagine.'

This dismissed any possibility that Dragomir's video might not be the real thing. But so was mine. I leaned back to the sofa, while he closed the video's window.

'Drago,' I said. 'If none of us is lying...' I couldn't finish the sentence. It was insane.

'...then we live in different times,' he said.

But no, as I easily verified, our timelines were similar to the day. Then, we checked several well known events and public developments. There were differences, not very important ones at first sight, but crucial enough to eventually segue into another world, where every large city embraced and welcomed other cities on a daily fight with intolerance.

Was it easy? No, Dragomir explained. The couplings created friction, in every participating city. Friction related to where they would take place, for how long they would last, to the welcome they would receive and extend themselves; to the past, to the military, financial or cultural conflicts. However, at the same time the couplings forced the city to be in constant contact with the *other*, that mysterious, up to yesterday distant, maybe even hostile other; and then the stranger got a face, became a woman with children, concerns or a job, a man stressed, in a hurry and with certain needs, a child in need of play, education and touch. Of course, you had those whose faces soured on both sides of the borders, those who feared the mixing of ideas more than they feared the mixing of the blood. They condemned, they warned, they threatened, but they rarely prevailed, even in terse situations with a sensitive past. Horrified, they watched people standing in front of the interface, dismissing the important issues. Most

Bulgarians didn't care to conquer the bay of Thermaikos, simple citizens of Skopje didn't hunger for the White Tower of Thessaloniki. The Albanians didn't dream of the Great Albania, the Turks didn't have plans for the Aegean islands or Thrace, just as most Greeks didn't live to enter Northern Epirus or Constantinople.

'Hmm, no, this is not the most accurate description,' Dragomir said. 'Some have such desires, and they consider them fair, but they are by no means the majority, and few of them would abandon their families and take up arms to make a reality of them, at least not without actual, targeted propaganda. However, it becomes more difficult to force propaganda on someone standing in front of the border. It's not that we realize the historical futility or the financial and social cost. It's that when you see another's baby inside its pram just a meter away from your own baby, you become less inclined to kill its father for a piece of land that at some point, for a certain stretch of time, used to belong to the grandfathers of your grandfathers—who, let us not forget ourselves, had chased away the grandfathers of someone else's grandfathers.' He cocked his head on the side and smiled. 'The couplings help. They don't, by any means, eliminate conflict and war, yet every day they make the clashes fewer, milder, shorter. They increase the collective empathy of the people. You should try them... *over there*,' he concluded.

That last word woke me up to the ominous reality. Slowly, I got up and straddled him on the sofa. I was afraid. I leaned in and kissed him, embraced him tight. We did not live in different time. We lived in different Athenses.

*

Yet, what was the possibility that two Athenses existed, so similar that they only differed in a few details, like the city couplings or the gentrification of a certain area, when we knew that there were already virtualities perfect in practically every detail, so hard to tell from the real thing? The procession of thought was relentless.

'One of us doesn't exist,' Dragomir whispered in my arms.

It was night, I only wore his shirt and we were sitting on the carpet drinking red wine. Through the glass bricks of the twenty-first floor at the Tower of Athens, we watched the slow, endless flow at Alexandra's Avenue and the Baghdad Square at its end. Not that it had, even unofficially, been given such a name, I was the one thinking of it this way.

'It is even worse,' I murmured.

It hadn't taken more than a few hours of research to stumble upon Nick Bostrom's simulation argument. A technologically mature civilization, Bostrom suggested, would have untold computing power. If even a small fraction of its people ran ancestor simulations, that are high fidelity simulations of their ancestors' lives, which the simulated ancestors themselves could not tell apart from reality, then the total sum of the simulated ancestors would be far greater than the total sum of the real ancestors.

'So at least one of the three following hypotheses is almost certainly true,' I said and held up a finger, separately from the others. 'The fraction of the cultures that are capable or running high fidelity ancestor simulations is close to zero.'

'Hmmm, this seems very likely, given that we are drinking our wine here in this place,' Dragomir said thoughtfully.

'Exactly.' I held up a second finger. 'The fraction of these civilizations interested in running such simulations is very close to zero.'

Dragomir shook his head slowly. 'Historians, psychologists and sociologists are anxious for every new development in the virtuality sector.'

I shook my head in bitter agreement, held up a third finger and took a deep breath. 'The fraction of all people sharing our kind of experiences living in a simulation is very close to one.'

Dragomir remained speechless for a couple of moments. 'None of us exists,' he stuttered. 'We are both virtual.'

'Yes,' I said. 'If so many people, with these capabilities, do run simulations of their ancestors, then the virtual people living inside those are so many, that the possibility of us living in reality is almost zero.'

'But... I feel real,' he said. 'As you definitely feel —'

'Hush,' I said, touching his knee. 'Let me show you how I feel.' I got up and returned to the bed, letting his shirt slide off me.

*

What is real? If you feel human, does it matter if you exist?

I stand in front of the statue of King Constantine the First, looking at grandmothers and loiterers. In my familiar Pedion Areos, without Baghdad Square, in my own world, whatever that means.

It must have been some inconsistency that allowed for the temporary communication between our worlds. Whether they are both virtual, or if any other combination is true, they were both coupled as if they were Athens and Baghdad. Maybe it was our own realization of the situation that caused the collapse of our coupling, maybe a warning light lit up out there, or maybe it was unintentional. In any case I did not see Dragomir again and the forum where I met him disappeared overnight.

As he saw me getting dressed for the last time, he told me he found nothing about Bostrom's Simulation Argument, even though he had researched a lot. That just the existence of this theory in one reality increased this reality's chances of being authentic, so I shouldn't worry, nobody was switching me off.

I don't know.

I don't know if someone switched Dragomir's Athens off. I hope that, if I do not think too hard about it, it will go away some years down the line.

I come here because there is no hotel room in the twenty-first floor of the Tower of Athens, and Phylis street is filled with brothels. I stand, I look at the grandmothers and the loiterers and wonder at how many Athenses there are. In one of them, a vicious battle might rage around the Votanikos mosque. In another, people might go to die at the Drapetsona necropolis. In a third one, the waters may have swept the beaches away. Or the city might be split in augmented reality zones, each one handled by a different guild. People might be separated in Citizens and Outsiders. Athenians might be wandering immigrants in the Humancity of Athens.

I don't know why I'm thinking of all this; it might be another inconsistency, or I might be pulling them out of thin air, because I cannot see the only Athens I would like to see: the one with the border of hope in it and the woman with the purple hijab greeting me with a smile at Baghdad Square.

The Bee Problem
Yiannis Papadopoulos & Stamatis Stamatopoulos

Translators from Greek: Dimitra Nikolaidou, Vaya Pseftaki

Market

'Hey, old man! You're the one fixing the bees?'

Nikitas dropped the peach he was holding on the merchant's stall, next to the other fruit, and turned towards the voice.

'What will you give us for those?' A little boy, hardly ten or twelve years old, grinned at him and held up a plastic opaque box in his outstretched hands. The boy was naked from the waist up, except for the backpack over his shoulders. Strips of pliable plastic were wrapped around his palms, crudely secured with duct tape. A few steps behind, a bunch of children looked at him with their mouths half-open. They were all wearing the characteristic makeshift *monkeys'* gloves.

Nikitas extended his right hand and lifted the lid of the box. There must have been more than thirty dead bee-drones in it. Not a bad haul.

'Who're you? New? Never seen you before,' he said to the boy.

The boy shook his head and flashed him an even wider grin. 'New. With Petr's gang. He sent us out today to test us, and if we do well, he said he'll let us go gather bees again. So? What will you give us?'

Nikitas took the box from the boy's hands and gestured for him to follow. It would be dusk soon, and the market was emptying. He found a deserted stall, laid the box on top and started counting drones.

'They're thirty seven. We counted them twice,' the boy said.

Nikitas glared at him and continued counting silently. Thirty seven. He blinked and felt the familiar tingling behind his right eyeball as his field of vision zoomed in. A quick examination showed some worn-down light-collectors and several mechanical damages in the hoverers. The usual. He shut the box, put it in his backpack and took out three oat biscuits. 'Thirty drones. Three biscuits,' he said and extended his hand, holding the trade-off.

'Hey, you're ripping us off! They're not thirty, they're-'

'If you don't like it, go elsewhere.'

'But you're the only one who buys drones.'

'Exactly.'

The children stood in hesitation for a while, mumbling to each other disgruntled, possibly bestowing all manner of curses upon him, but Nikitas couldn't care less. Both himself and the monkeys that provided him with drones now and then, either for repairs or for reprogramming, knew that he was the only one in Saint Lucas collective who knew how to handle, fix and program bee-drones.

The boy that had brought the box reached out and took the biscuits, and all together, they ran up Karavia street. In the Patmos farm, they grabbed the ropes one after the other and he saw them climbing up fast towards the orangeries. One of the children paused, hovered with just one hand, brought the other to his mouth forming a funnel and shouted: 'Now that the bees are coming back, we won't need you any more, you old skinflint!'

Nikitas scoffed. The little buggers would say anything to nettle him. Bees, go figure! The only place he knew of where living bees existed, was the New Belgian Natural History Museum in the Central Sector of Athens. Nevertheless, the thought was galling; his work for the collective, his own survival, depended on the fact that bees had essentially become extinct decades ago.

He left Karavia market and stepped into Samara street. He hovered over the Nigerians' stalls just in case he found a decent spare part for his hand. The last few days it glitched a lot, and he feared that it would break down on him. The Africans rarely had something of value, but when he did find anything, it was the good stuff. Only those sons of bitches, the Pakis, managed to maintain a steady flow of spare parts. He went on and turned right on Pammakaristos Church until he reached his workshop. A semi-basement that stank but at least didn't get damp. He had repeatedly asked the assembly for a better place, but they kept ignoring him. That's how things are. He held them by the neck with the bee-drones that were necessary for the pollination, and they had him by the balls offering him security: they let him stay with them, far from the patrols of his former colleagues in Central Section. How degrading. A former cop, even if just a technician, under the protection of anarchists and their illegal migrant friends.

'Start-up, Nikitas. Four, three, lamda,' he said, but the monitors covering the walls of the semi-basement remained dark. He repeated the password to no avail. Inflow problems? Nine out of ten times, some little bastard stole the wires or the whole solar panel from the terrace. And what did they do to them when they caught them? Obligatory work in the infrastructure. But if he sneezed the wrong way, they would kick him to the first control gate of the central sector. 'Fuck my luck,' he groaned and right before he stepped out, he caught a glimpse of the stand-by indicator blinking slowly on Lydia's work station. So, the inflow was okay. He approached his counter and bent over the power supply unit of his station. The faint smell of something burnt.

Before he had time to curse, the door banged open and Lydia rushed in the workshop. Sweaty and flushed, she bumped on him.

'Where have you been? How many times have I told you not to leave your system running when you're out? Huh? How many more times should I have to tell you?' he yelled at her.

The girl froze, terrified, and Nikitas felt a small pang in his stomach. Lydia was only twelve years old and unfortunately, *or fortunately*, his only company. She had latched onto him three years ago, when she'd tried to sell him a broken bee-drone. The drone was is such condition that none of the monkeys would have brought it to him. But Lydia had something entirely different on her mind. She wasn't interested in trapping the flying things. She wanted to learn how to repair them, to make them fly again. Now, Nikitas wasn't sure whether he had decided to teach her everything he knew because she was a natural at programming or because he needed someone around, even if this someone was just a child.

Something deep inside pushed him to admit that the girl was part of the redemption he sought, for the sake of the little boy he watched bleeding out on his live feed five years ago. The thought brought him round and at the same time riled him. Guilt was not a good thing. It had led him to this shitty community.

'I don't know how much longer I'll be able to put up with you,' he said. 'You've started getting-'

Instead of answering, Lydia raised her hand and showed him a small transparent bag she was holding by its corner.

'Look what I found!'

He took the bag from the girl and emptied its contents in his palm. He gawped at the two insects. He might have never seen them before in his life, but the compound eyes, the transparent wings and the yellow-grey, fuzzy body didn't leave much room for doubt. He pressed the still soft bodies with his finger and finally returned the dead bees to Lydia.

'I found them in the Afghans' crops. And there are rumours of beehives. That we might be able to use these new bees for pollination. That-'

Nikitas raised his hand. 'All right. Got it,' he roared. He brought his hand to his head pretending to smooth his hair out, spun around and nailed his eyes on Lydia's system. He took a small bunch of folded papers out of his pockets, sorted out two and gave them to Lydia.

'Run down to the Pakis. I need a new 7.5 power supply adapter and I need it yesterday. These coupons are good for three of them.'

The girl opened her mouth to speak.

'Go!' he said.

Beekeeper

Nikitas walked on the street with his head down and his hands in his pockets. This whole thing was not good. Not good at all. Living bees in the community? Not good, not one bit. All he had that allowed him to coexist with this bunch of anarchists, hippies and potheads was this leverage. But the two yellow-grey bodies along with the rumours the girl had told him about could change everything—if they hadn't already.

He took a left in Defkalionos. At the corner on his left, something that looked like an old super market had been converted into a coolhouse, and lemon trees, orange trees and dwarf apple trees were visible behind the power-producing crystals, safely secured away from the heat. Right outside, under the shade from the block of flats' balconies, the pavement's tiles had been removed so they could plant tomatoes and beans.

A few metres down the road, he entered a neoclassical building and crossed a half-dark corridor. On the opposite side, the noon's glare struggled to creep in from an open door. He went out again, under the heat of the sun, to the backyard, and sat on one of the few tables that were arranged under a large pine tree.

The first thing he did after he sent Lydia to fetch a power supply adapter for his system, was to get down to business. His old, familiar business, thanks to which he wasn't, let's say, one of the favourites in Saint Lucas. SSR: Search-Surveillance-Recording. It took him all night, but until first light he had prepared a small swarm of search drones programmed to locate living bees and then survey and record areas with high concentration of the damned insects. With a little luck, he would quickly find the hives, or whatever their nests were called, and whoever took care of them. Normally, the only thing he had to do now was wait for the search results and the first recordings. Sooner or later he would have the information he needed. He didn't have the luxury of time though. For all he knew his place in the community was already compromised. He didn't take their preaching about cooperation, solidarity, non-vindictive correction and whatever

pompous and incomprehensible shit they always talked about in
their assemblies at face value. He was certain: at the very first
opportunity, the *copper* would go back where he came from.

When Lydia returned empty-handed from the Pakis, he let
her in on the ploy. 'Forget about the power supply. Ask, find
out, bring me information on the bees and you will have two
18 core processors for your farm on the same day. Plus the
holograph you've been asking for.' The girl left running. Strange
child. You gave her a sweet and she would spit it out. You gave
her a computer chip and she would jump around excited. As it
finally turned out, his tactic bore fruit. There had already been
two days and nights in his workshop, with precious little sleep,
writing filter routines for the recordings the drones sent, and his
eyes stung treacherously from the simultaneous scanning. So far,
the drones sent stray images of bees in various farms of Saint
Lucas, but they hadn't managed to lock on an insect and follow it
to its hive. Nikitas was sick of watching videos with the fucking
insects flying from plant to plant, among happy-go-lucky farmers.
The prospect of being able to ditch the community before its
members decided that he was useless had started playing on his
numb mind when Lydia came back with news.

'There's a new guy. Palestinian or Syrian or something like it.
You know, an Arab. He's training them.'

Nikitas paused the video he was watching and turned to the
girl. 'Training them? What do you mean?'

Lydia shrugged and collapsed on the threadbare couch that
Nikitas used for his afternoon nap. She sighed and grimaced in
relief as she tried to get rid of her combat boots with her feet. 'I
don't know. That's what I understood. That he's training them,'
she said.

'Who is he? What's his name? Where does he live?'

Lydia began to shrug again, but her eyes widened and focused
on the monitors behind Nikitas. She sprang up, stumbled on the
half-worn combat boot, reached out, pointed and shouted: 'She!
She knows!'

Nikitas turned and looked at the screen. A woman around
thirty, squatting in between rows of sprouts. She was wearing a

military overall with cut-off trouser legs and sleeves, while a scarf was wrapped around her neck. She was skinny and her hair—at least what she had left on her half-shaven skull—fluoresced between light green and blue, and was, in a manner of speaking, wrapped on the top of her head. She wore dark sunglasses; mandatory accessory to battle the sunlight. Nikitas hadn't seen her before.

'Who's she? You know her?'

'Her name's Christina and she's one of those in charge of the vertical Italian-school crops.'

So now, Nikitas was sitting in the yard of the Dutchman's coffee shop. He'd never been here before. Who would he come with, anyway? Even so, it was a well-known meeting place and since Lydia claimed that Christina came here every afternoon, and as of late always with a newcomer that looked like an Arab, it was due time to pay a visit.

She was there. In her cut-off overalls and her colourful hair, only that now she wore it down. She spoke excitedly with the two men who were sitting at the same table and every now and then she laughed out loud. He knew one of them. The Dutchman. That's what they all called him even if he wasn't the only Dutch living in the community. It was said that he lived in Greece many years before the first north-western Europe floods; he wasn't among those who had come with the relocation programs. It made sense, since most of them didn't choose the collectives; they relocated in the best spots of Greece, with their expensive cars, their robotic servants and their lofty gaze. At least they had brought their jobs with them and didn't suck Greece dry, as did the millions that swarmed about the Balkans in the beginning of the century, after the Middle East wars.

The third person of the company, judging by his dark complexion and accent, must have been the Arab.

There weren't many ways to do that, so he started improvising lines and excuses in order to approach them and chat them up, while he was watching Christina talk with them. He had no idea what he could say. He had nothing to do with these people. He belonged to a totally different world, a world based on rules, order, decency. Once more, he felt appalled with himself and the situation he had ended up in. Hunted by his own, forced to live here, among this lot.

As it turned out, to his great relief, he didn't have to do anything.

The Dutchman got up from his chair and approached him. He greeted him with a nod and said: 'I just opened a new barrel of lager. Should I get you some? Or are you expecting company?'

Nikitas started to answer, but the Dutchman went on.

'You're Nikitas, aren't you?'

Nikitas nodded.

'The drone guy.'

'Yes. The drone guy,' Nikitas said forcing a smile.

The Dutchman turned to his company and said loudly: 'Christina! You'll never guess who's here!' Then, he turned to Nikitas and gestured at him to get up and follow him. Seconds later, they were all sitting around the same table.

'Hi, I'm Christina.' She smiled.

Nikitas couldn't help feeling awkward; big eyes that looked straight into his, none of them saying *hello, cop*. He wondered whether the Arab was fucking her.

'Akhram, this is Nikitas, the one I was telling you about. Isn't this a great coincidence?' And right away to Nikitas: 'Akhram and you are colleagues, in a way.'

Akhram laughed and extended his hand to Nikitas: 'Nice to meet you.'

Nikitas hesitated. He wiped his palm on his trousers and extended his too. He shook Akram's hand and answered with just a nod.

It was all true.

Akhram had arrived at the community from Palestine a few weeks ago, bringing along two beehives with living bees. How he got them was not clear, but what proved crystal clear was his knowledge of them, even though he didn't want to be acknowledged as a beekeeper.

'Unfortunately,' he said, 'what's lost along with the bees is the expertise. What I know comes out of personal interest and study. But it's worth a try. Maybe one day, bees will become again an active part of the cycle of nature.'

Akhram didn't stay with them for long. 'I have to go. I'm sure we'll talk again though. Christina will explain to you.'

'Kiss Ashil for me!' Christina said as she waved him goodbye.

So he wasn't fucking her. Although you should expect anything from their lot.

He had no reason to stay longer. He had learned whatever he needed, but, even with some small amount of guilt, to some extent he enjoyed the conversation with Christina. Besides, if he hadn't gone forward himself, they would have looked for him anyway. The reason? He couldn't help but smile on the inside.

'We thought,' Christina said, 'that the only two people in our collectivity who know even a little about bees and how exactly they work are you and Akhram.'

Did they take him for such a fool? If Akhram managed to maintain the beehives, and even worse, to make the bees productive as far as crop pollination was concerned, then what would be Nikitas' job in the community? None, of course. They wouldn't need his bee-drones any more.

'Yes, sure. If there's anything I can do.' He hesitated for a bit and added: 'Although, as you said, I don't have any specialised knowledge. I don't see how I could help you. Or Akhram.'

'You can help. Isn't it how this place exists anyway?' Christina said. 'We face problems each and every day. But we're there for each other, we're willing to be part of the solution. Look around. It's no small feat what we've accomplished here. Is it? And few of us are experts in anything. It's a fight.'

Nikitas chose not to answer. For a few moments, he allowed himself to notice Christina's smile—even though she was so skinny, he had to admit that she was charming. Then he stood up, said goodbye and went out under the scorching midday sun, trying to put his thoughts in order. They always spiraled down to the same image: some former colleague of his holding him still, while another handcuffed him.

Fire

His drones didn't let him down. Just the following night, he received pictures from the Italian school's crops; the two blue boxes that had carefully been set up under a makeshift, wooden shade on the terrace of the building were certainly beehives. There was one last thing to do. He stretched his arms and started writing on the old style keyboard in front of him.

Nikitas always considered himself a man of reason. He understood that nothing good ever came out of the crowds of foreigners that had settled—and still poured into—Greece. Crime, unemployment, dirt, even contagious diseases, they were all their fault, or they were at least the side-effects of their presence in his country. This all may have started by the end of the last century, and grown huge now, possibly irreversibly, but it didn't mean that he himself didn't see it and that he wouldn't try to do anything he could to change it. So he applied for and joined the European Control and Investigation Corps for Illegal Movement and Immigration. The work they'd been conducting there was absolutely necessary and he didn't feel bad about it at all. His specialty as a surveillance drone technician always kept him away from the field. Illegal immigrants were digits, numbers and wretched faces that had to be registered in the system for processing. Between him and his colleagues' raids in customs, ports, hidden cargo holds and shitholes that stunk of sweat, sick breath and piss, there was static noise and the live feed's bad image quality.

Except for that one time.

He had never managed to clear up inside him what was to blame. Maybe there was something in the boy's look shortly before the bullets penetrated his chest. But the mistake was made. Reason yielded, Nikitas refused to cover it up and leaked images of the six year old illegal immigrant's execution. Of course, he was immediately suspended and then a series of arrest warrants were issued, for 'crimes against the citizens of the European Republic.'

And here he was. A fugitive.

Life in Saint Lucas was not the best, but he didn't intend to end up in prison. The only safety measure he had were the bee-drones and the lack of real bees.

There wasn't much to be done now. He had taken every measure he could to prevent any possible correlation of his drones to the accident. It was past midnight when he locked the workshop and headed down to the Dutch's coffee shop. Besides, it was the only place he knew that never closed.

An hour later, he heard the first screams. Then the sound of running, winded talk, and in the end, he thought he heard crying.

'Fire!'

'…at the Italian crops.'

'…alive. They got burned alive!'

Assembly

From what he knew, fire victims rarely get burned before they die. They are usually spared the suffering because they have already choked to death—or something like it. Anyhow, Akhram and Christina were dead. They found them in the crops' ground floor. What were they doing in the crops at night? Had they seen the fire and tried to save the bees? He would never find out. No one would.

He found himself in the assembly, standing at the back, with his eyes nailed on the young girl—four? Five?—who, all this time, sat silent and still on an assembly coordinator's lap. There was mayhem, and the acoustics of the old church that now functioned as a general assembly hall, wasn't helping. Nikitas rarely attended these procedures that lasted for too long and in his opinion were ineffective, energy draining and most times hit a dead-end. Exactly like today. The dead wouldn't come back.

He was trying to remember how he had woken up this morning, if he had slept the night before, if he had helped put out the fire or whether he had crawled back to his hole, among the wires and the monotonous, hypnotic buzz of his computers. He tried to remember if it was him who compulsively counted his drones, in order to make sure that none were missing, if it was him who frantically rubbed the tiny flying things, cleaning them of dirt, of every possible, imaginary or real, black, guilty soot, or whether it was someone else, some evil self of his, drawn out of a nightmare. He tried to remember whether he had removed the flight routines from the terminal or whether the metallic tips that dug into the skin of his clenched, sweaty palm, in his pocket, were the antennae and the legs of the drones that he should have stashed away.

He clenched his teeth until his jaw hurt. There was a hammering at his temples.

The dead won't come back.

He unclenched his palm in his pocket and focused again on what was said around him. He had to know what information had been out, whether they had suspicions, what steps they would take, whether they would conduct an investigation and in what direction. And above all: would his name be heard in connection to the two dead and the destroyed beehives?

The sickly pale blonde—she introduced herself as Christina's coworker—that had started talking was just another voice that didn't offer any kind of solution. Too much talk and no substance.

'This issue,' she said, 'has nothing to do with the bees.' A small protestation followed her words and then the two-three voices became ten, and soon a coordinator had to intervene and the blonde's voice was heard a little louder now. 'We will manage without them. We don't need them. We have solutions. Yes, it would be good and useful, maybe, if we managed to restore them back to the plants' natural reproductive cycle, but it was a long shot right from the start. Christina knew that, Akhram knew that. We couldn't depend on them. Today's issue is a different one.'

She stopped, looked at the little girl and said: 'This is Akhram's daughter, Ashil.'

His limbs went numb, all sound faded replaced by the high pitched tone of drilling deep into his head. Nikitas could see people around him raising their hands, talking. Someone seemed to shout. In the heat of the cramped hall of the church, he was sweating, like everyone, but his sweat was cold. It made his eyes sting, but he wouldn't close them, because every time he did, Ashil's afterimage transformed into the little boy who had been murdered by his colleagues a few years ago. Even worse were the questions rising up in his mind. Would he have stopped the drones, if he knew that Akhram had a daughter, or if he knew that Akhram and Christina would be at the crops that night? Would he have changed his mind?

Nikitas shut his eyes and shook his head.

'Me.' His voice sounded like a stranger's in his ears. The uproar rushed back violently. No one seemed to have heard him. Aware of the sounds around him once more he raised his hands, shouted 'Me!' at the top of his lungs and started walking towards the centre of the church. The voices subsided and they all stood staring at him in silence. Many must have recognized him, but none of them had ever seen him here before, among them, and this alone was enough to make them all hush. Nikitas reached the middle of the church and felt everyone's eyes fixed on him, burning.

Come on, say it.

'Me.'

They would turn him in to the Central Sector and he would pay the bitter price. *Yes, a bitter price indeed*, not because he'd burned two people, but because he'd blown the lid off an unjustifiable murder. He caught himself smiling bitterly at the irony.

At best, they would keep him here and sentence him to one of their stupid, painless disciplinary actions. He almost burst out laughing. He wanted to confess that he was guilty, but he would never get the punishment he deserved. These people had no idea how to punish, they didn't have the balls for it. Even now, they didn't care to find out who was responsible for the death of two people, they were just looking for someone to pass the girl to.

Yes, you moron, because that's the point. And the solution.

That's the punishment.

'Me,' he said. 'I will take Akhram's place.'

T2
Kelly Theodorakopoulou

Translators from Greek: Dimitra Nikolaidou, Vaya Pseftaki

Erietta-Natalia stood in front of the mirror-fitted column at the pier, scrunching her nose. The colour of her hair which, following the extravagantly priced dye job changed with the light, from a metallic cobalt blue to dark purple to light fuchsia-gold with white streaks, now looked like a blunt aubergine-grey under the sparse sunrays that managed to shove themselves into the electric railway station. She sighed and shook her head, turning her gaze at the electronic sign which displayed the routes' timetable.

KIFISIA: 8 (T1)

She pulled her eyes from there and mumbled: 'We should have taken the dirty one.'

'But Erna!' Alexandros-Philippos turned to look at her in shock, which swaddled her from the edge of her loose white blouse up to her face.

'Come on, Aleph!' she jerked her shoulder. 'The fact that they charge double for the ticket doesn't mean it's better.'

'But, they say that they clean it up with eco-friendly detergents twice a day, they paint the walls more often and they change the seats' fabric.'

'That's what the ad says. Yet it also said it would be as frequent as the dirty one, and there goes that claim.'

Alexandros-Philippos opened his mouth to object, but then he remembered how easily their last talk about money had ended up in a fight, and thus swallowed his tongue. As if trying to convince himself to change the subject, he turned to look at the other people standing on the pier. It was easy to guess who among them was waiting for the clean train, T1, and who was waiting for T2. The gentleman with the tie and the attaché case would have obviously purchased the double ticket, so his suit would not need a dry cleaner the next day. The woman with the scruffy shoes and the scarf wrapped around her head would have probably considered the increased fare a useless luxury. As for the young man in the threadbare t-shirt, the stained trousers and the vacant stare, Alexandros-Philippos doubted if he could even afford the cheap fare. Only the girl with the long dark skirt, the graffiti t-shirt, the tote bag full of badges, with a book in hand and a blue streak in her hair, made Alexandros-Philippos hesitate. Yet before he had to force his facial muscles to remain empty of every objectionable expression, he heard a thud right behind him and turned, startled.

A woman, who had been lying motionless on a bench all that time, had slipped and fallen down, and nobody was going near her. Her ancient frilly, patterned blouse, her jeans, faded and torn through use rather than by design, her rough hands and the wrinkles on her unpainted face made the suited ladies scan the safe distance between them.

In the seconds left before T1 arrived, Alexandros-Philippos and Erietta-Natalia wouldn't have enough time to do anything for the stranger, even if they intended to. Yet the relief that the train was saving them from the awkward moment manifested on Erietta-Natalia's face alone. Alexandros-Phlippos had been carried away watching through the train's window the girl with the long skirt and the blue streak kneeling by the fallen woman and placing her tote bag under her head. He thought that he would never find out which of the two trains the girl was waiting for, after all. And then the answer seemed so obvious, that he wondered to himself—how had it even crossed his mind that someone like her would ever choose to take the T1.

In the somehow ostentatiously clean carriage, with the white fluorescent surfaces and the vivid colours even on the ads, all the passengers, despite their indifferent expression, gave the impression that they wore new clothes, unworn until today, like uniforms without which they wouldn't be allowed onboard. Or rather, almost all of them.

Erietta-Natalia pointed with her head and whispered to him: 'Will you still want me, if I become like her?'

'Alexandros-Philippos noticed, somehow startled, that her voice sounded only in part coy, joking. For a minute he thought that Erietta-Natalia meant the woman they had seen tumbling from the bench onto the pier. However, when he turned to look at where she was pointing, his expression changed.

He knew, of course, that despite the increased frequency of ticket inspections aboard the T1 compared to the T2, there were always those who came onboard without paying, but their sight, or rather the contrast between their looks and the other passengers, had never ceased to shock him.

'Good evening, ladies and gentlemen, I'm not a beggar, I'm the mother of two who lost her job eighteen months ago, and I'm selling these tissues to get by. I'm not asking for charity…'

Incapable of stopping his brow and cheeks from crinkling reflexively, Alexandros-Philippos rummaged through his memory to see if he had ever met someone of this age and gender under these circumstances before. She was a woman not much older than Erietta-Natalia. Yet it took a lot of imagination for someone to even flittingly think that those two had something in common: the skin on this one's face and hands looked like dry hide, there were white streaks in her oily hair, her teeth… Alexandros-Philippos peeled his eyes away as if asphyxiating. He let them rest on Erietta-Natalia, her shiny ponytail, her creamy skin, her soft golden eyelashes, her lips that looked 'as if a rose had bloomed there,' as he used to text her when they first started dating. He tried to drive away the uninvited memory that, as of late, among her cosmetics apart from the jars and tubes, a few syringes and pills had made their appearance. Of course, she herself said that she didn't use anything and that she had just bought them because it was a bargain, but Alexandros-Philippos hadn't checked to see if their wrappings had been opened since he'd first noticed them.

He looked at her ambiguously, but her gaze, still looking for an answer, brought him back to reality like the prick of a pin.

'Ugh, what do you want me to say, appearance is not the most important thing,' he managed to messily utter the clichéd expression of so many ads and movies.

'Yes, but,' Erietta-Natalia shifted her position and turned towards him without smiling, 'don't they say that sixty percent of a relationship lies in the sex? Which means in,' she nailed her eyes on him, 'appearance.'

Alexandros-Philippos glanced at the map of the stops above the door: no, the end of their route was still far away, arrival would not save him. But suddenly, he lacked an appetite to look for more elaborate excuses.

'Come on now, don't get stressed,' he put his arm around her shoulders. 'You're a doll.'

Erietta-Natalia, as if regretting that she had started such a conversation, rested her head on his shoulder like a cat, and they remained like that till a seat was empty.

'Kifisia. Final stop. Passengers are kindly requested to disembark.'

This voice, always the same... Alexandros-Philippos remembered a conversation he had overheard not so long ago, again inside the electric train: a girl, no more than ten, had asked her mom whether, when the train lines had been separated to T1 and T2, they had also recorded a new voice for the announcements of the 'clean' one and, upon getting a negative answer, had frowned and nagged that it wasn't nice at all to let the passenger who held the double-priced tickets listening to the voice of a dead lady. Alexandros-Philippos opened his mouth to relay this memory to Erietta-Natalia, but she had already gotten up as soon as the train stopped and was jostling for the door.

Before a smile had spread itself on Erietta-Natalia's face, now that the sunlight had turned her hair colour to an impressive silver-purple, her eyes fell upon the edge of the square opposite her, and her expression froze.

'Aleph... what's going on here?'

The whole of the Kifisia Grove and the streets around the

square were flooded with people, who had their backs turned to Erietta-Natalia and were shouting slogans in languages unknown to her. What's more, they showed no intention of moving on and their outfits, at least the outfits of the ones in the back, those closest to her field of vision, made her assume they must have taken T2 to get here. Lost, she looked at the other passengers who, upon exiting the carriage, either entered cars directly or backtracked and delved into the station to find the downstairs exit.

Alexandros-Philippos appeared behind Erietta-Natalia, scrunching his eyebrows together. 'Muslim protest requesting a mosque. I think I'd read something the other day, but I forgot about it.'

'But...' Erietta-Natalia made a vague hand gesture. 'How're we going to get through?'

'Weren't you the one saying we should take the dirty one, only minutes ago?' Alexandros-Philippos cast a side glance at her, raising his eyebrow.

'To tell you off about the money, Aleph, I wasn't being serious!' Erietta-Natalia looked desperate, in part for his stupidity in not understanding that and in part for the dead-end of their situation.

'It's OK, we will walk around them, it's no big deal. After all, the doctor's office is not on the square.'

'...so that any of them can jump us in an alley and just shoot us without anyone finding out, especially now that they are set up to fight with Greeks.'

'In plain daylight, and in the Northern suburbs?' Alexandros-Philippos turned to examine Erietta-Natalia to make sure that she meant what she was saying and wasn't just being a contrarian, but he couldn't tell.

'Perhaps we should call the doctor and cancel?' Her look was the perfect imitation of innocence and fear.

'No, Erna! He will reschedule us two months from now!' He grabbed her arm and they started walking towards their left, turning their backs to the square. As Alexandros-Philippos mumbled and swore through his teeth trying to find a detour for the same destination, he didn't notice her own triumphantly malicious smile.

Only when they reached the entrance of the building with the bronze plaque *I. G. Melekos, Gynecologist* above the doorbells, pressed the button and heard the buzzer, Erietta-Natalia's face began to soften. Even when the doctor asked her to raise her blouse and spread on her belly the cold gel that made the ultrasound's nozzle glide more easily, she remained unperturbed, strengthening Alexandros-Philippos' suspicions that the ruckus she had raised the first time was all coyness and theatrics. He, on the other hand, needed to hold himself back not to show how annoyed he was by the doctor's display of wealth: not only was the office decorated with pieces more expensive than tasteful, especially these abstract sculptures made of non-recognizable, strangely coloured ores which were in vogue as of late, but also I G. Melekos himself had violet eyes. Which meant that he had bought the last generation of contact lenses, those that had colour and still didn't hinder vision at all. Violet lenses were available in this iteration only and the few pieces that had circulated were way too expensive—Alexandros-Philippos had heard the actor who played Drizzt Do'Urden say so in a YouTube interview.

'Everything is fine.' The doctor said so to the air, his hand on the nozzle's handle and his eyes on the machine's screen. 'It's too early of course, but the embryo's development is normal, there's no reason to worry... as to that.'

'As to that.' Erietta-Natalia repeated the last sentence raising her head to look at him and, for the first time since entering his office, her face creased. 'As to that, there is no reason to worry. You mean there is reason to worry as to something else?'

'Eh.' I. G Melekos turned to her, opened his mouth, shut it before settling on what to say, and in the end came to a decision: 'It's not a matter of health. It's just that the results of the prenatal DNA test came out and it's something that... anyhow, I will tell you and you get to be the judges.'

Toweling the gel off Erietta-Natalia's belly, getting dressed and getting to the doctor's desk took a little longer than normal; the hands of the girl with the multicoloured hair were trembling.

'Don't be like that!' The tone which the doctor used to calm her down was completely fake: he seemed more annoyed at her agitation than sorry for her. 'It's just that the test showed that the appearance of your baby will have a characteristic that is… let us say, 'non-ideal'.'

'What? Will it be too short? I had an uncle who…' Alexandros-Philippos took pity on her and bravely intervened, to rescue her from guilt.

'No, not that.'

'Will it be predisposed towards obesity? My mother used to say that…'

'But I told you: this has nothing to do with health.'

'Then?' Alexandros-Phillpos weighed for a moment the possibility of getting angry.

I. G. Melekos distanced his body from the desk to say:

'Your baby will be born with brown eyes.'

It was as if the words signaled for the tension to slide off Alexandros-Philippos and Erietta-Natalia like a too-large cloak, and they turned to each other startled. Unconsciously they rummaged through their memory for the last brown-eyed people they had seen, and the realization made them shift in their chairs: they were the passengers of T2. Alexandros-Philippos had enough composure to go even farther back and remember that both his parents belonged to this category but this wasn't enough to calm him. When he spoke, his voice came out upset:

'So what? Isn't it the most common colour among the Greeks?'

'Not anymore.' The doctor nodded his head towards their own faces: her eyes were green and his were grey-blue. 'To be precise, following the mixings with immigrants in the latest decades, the upper classes have procreated with Eastern European women, so we have fair colours, while the dark ones usually come from Middle Eastern families, which came here and became Greeks themselves.'

Became Greeks so to speak, Alexandros-Philippos wanted to say as he remembered the protest at the Kifisias Grove, but he held himself back and said nothing, because he was less interested in this conversation than he was in another one. 'And what does it matter?'

I. G. Melekos spread his hands with the look of a scientist presenting fragments of his wisdom so that others could make a decision without his interference. 'Decades ago, research conducted in America found out that those who had ugly, cacophonous, unpopular names, lived on average nine years less than the rest. Today, this gap has tripled.'

'But we still don't have that….' Erietta-Natalia didn't have the patience to go through irrelevant examples to get to the point, but Alexandros-Philippos gave her a reassuring glance.

'Similarly, statistics say that today, those who hold high positions in the hierarchy of employment as well as greater wealth, do not possess brown eyes by 83%.'

'But…!'

'And ten years ago, the number was 70%.'

'Which means that in ten years…' Erietta-Natalia's look showed that the doctor had managed to convey the anxiety he was aiming for. He cast a side glance at Alexandros-Philippos but he didn't immediately find the words needed to convince him too.

'So what?' he said, shrugging. 'Even if we accept that it's important, there's nothing we can do about it. Can we?' He turned to look at the doctor provocatively.

'There is a pill that influences such small DNA details…' he began hesitantly.

And costs as much as both our salaries for six months! Alexandros-Philippos nearly threw that out like the lid of a pot full of steam, but a glance from Erietta-Natalia stopped him.

'…but I would suggest, as a less costly solution,' and at this phrase his violet eyes assumed a politely disdainful expression, 'to take advantage of the fact that you are one of the few couples coming to my practice without any fertility problems, terminate the pregnancy and try again.'

Alexandros-Philippos' mouth slacked open. He turned to Erietta-Natalia, and the fact that she didn't have an equally startled look on her face made his blood boil. His wife though took his hand and stopped him before he spoke.

'Thank you, doctor. Anything else?'

'Here,' the man with the violet eyes took an envelope from the drawer and gave it to her, 'the test results, if you're looking for another opinion. Have a good day.'

*

'He's a madman, there's no other explanation! We should go to someone else.' Even before the glass entrance door of the building was shut behind him, right in front of the *I.G. Melekos, Gynecologist* plaque, Alexandros-Philippos shook his head angrily and stepped on the street, with Erietta-Natalia following him.

'Yes, it sounds excessive, but Aleph, think. Will it have the money to buy the most expensive contact lenses, for the rest of its life? Even if they get cheaper meanwhile... The child itself will accuse us at some point, for burdening it with such a useless expense. They used to send them at tutoring sessions, foreign languages and music schools to remove another characteristic right from the start, for instance illiteracy, or ignorance. Now it is just a different time and... Come on, stop running, I'll fall on my face trying to catch up with you. Stop and let us talk about it, don't behave like a savage!'

'Oh, I am the one behaving like a...? Fine, Erna!'

They were so upset that they forgot to return to the station through the same detour they had taken earlier on, so they went through the square. However, the protest had now ended and the Kifisias Grove was almost deserted, so much so that the two of them didn't realize their mistake. Only some pamphlets, written in a foreign language, flew in front of them, scattered by the wind.

Those We Serve
Eugenia Triantafyllou

The image came to Manoli when he switched to his summer settings. It had become his secret ritual. Summer always began with Amelia. Hers was his most vivid memory.

In that memory, Amelia had a round, youthful face laced with a toothy smile and wore her brown hair in a high ponytail. It was hot and humid and they were by the pool bar, their clothes sticky against their skin. In that memory he was human.

He wanted the image to linger a little longer, lying inside his podbed, but his spine had already started to complain. The pinging on the back of his skull was dull but insistent.

The island above was slightly askew.

An earthquake, 4.2 on the Richter scale. Not a threat, but still needing his attention. He imagined Amelia walking between crumbled buildings, disoriented, lost and it was enough to make him leave his pod.

Thankfully the damage was minimal. As he took his skin out of cryostorage and layered it meticulously on his steel chassis he calculated the shifting on the surface. No ground displacement and minor subsidence in a couple of areas. The island would crumble to dust eventually, but it wasn't going to be today.

This time of the year the island of Santo flooded with tourists. Ships arrived at the docks by the dozens, people engulfed the streets, shoulders bumped against shoulders, brushed against the whitewashed walls of cubic houses, bodies squeezed themselves a bit too tight through narrow alleyways.

The waves of people smashed against the already derelict

buildings yet were tamer each year. There were other things to do now, other places to visit. So each year the crowd dwindled. Unlike him, the tourists were free to leave.

Manoli would always be at the reception, expecting them summer after summer, smiling and greeting politely. They didn't know it wasn't really him they met at the Heliotrope Hotel. He was just an artificial, an illegal copy of the original. His existence was punishable by law. He was a summer-only person and summer was all he had to live for. The real him, the human Manoli, lived in the city of Santo, under the sea.

*

At the Heliotrope's lobby, Manoli bumped into the winter staff retreating underground. They nodded at him and transferred some useful information about the weather and the outside world but did not talk much. There wasn't anything to talk about. The winter staff seemed strange even to him. During the winter the island was completely stripped of outside stimuli, except for the occasional surprise visits from humans which winter-persons handled in an admittedly unfriendly manner. It was cold and empty and tomb-silent. That's why the winter-persons were so few, so sullen, and their eyes seemed unfocused at times. Manoli wanted to thank them but preferred not to stare at them for too long.

When he stood behind the counter Manoli hesitated for a moment but turned on the feed of the island's traffic cameras.

A crystal-clear image materialized over his optic sensors. His eyes jumped from port view to airport, to street and back, searching among the many faces of the tourists the one that interested him. He was able to recognize some regulars; recall their faces from the artificials' databank.

Amelia was nowhere to be found. She was supposed to arrive today. By now he had run through all the available feeds a hundred times each and the realization that she might have not made it this year had started to settle on him like the thick layer of dust on his old podbed during wintertime.

He sighed. Amelia had booked a room at the Heliotrope several months before and he never received a cancellation message, but humans were unpredictable. Amelia had canceled three times before. The first time when Amelia went to college and she missed several summers travelling to other parts of the world, then her honeymoon in the Bahamas and just last summer was the divorce.

The stubby silhouette of the bus driver Panos arrived at the counter. He was saddled with suitcases, handbags, and satchels, as he plodded along the marble floor behind two women who were chatting and snapping photos of the surroundings. Manoli looked around for Amelia but she was not with them either.

Panos's right fist was curled around what could only be money, coins and bills.

'You should leave those here,' Manoli said softly as he approached. Panos turned around as the elevator doors slid open. The women got in, still chatting and the doors closed behind them. None of them noticed Panos did not follow.

Panos's face scrunched up into a scowl. Manoli knew his friend liked keeping tips. It made him feel real and anachronistic, like the island. Panos favored pennies because they were a useless piece of metal.

'Like we are,' he would joke with Manoli as he made them clink against the jug he kept under his driver's seat. 'But they won't be when I have enough to buy this island.'

Manoli would say nothing because the pennies were already a part of the island once the tourists offered them. And the artificials were part of the island too. They could not buy anything ever. But of course Panos did not care about such realities. The human Panos must have been a dreamer as well.

Manoli looked at his open palm and then at Panos. He sighed and gave Manoli the bills.

'I am keeping the pennies. It's not like they'll ever come up here for the tips,' he muttered and yanked the suitcases behind him.

'Be careful, brother,' Manoli said. 'We don't want unhappy customers.' The pennies bothered him but he chose to ignore it.

Panos groaned but hauled the luggage more carefully. When the elevator door opened, he winked at Manoli and disappeared behind the sliding doors.

Manoli grabbed the metallic box from behind the counter, took the rubber band off the bundle of money and wrapped the new bills with the rest. Some of them had already expired and were worthless. It didn't matter. He was responsible for them as for everything else on the island. Soon he would have to take them to the safe downstairs.

Nobody came for this money. It was slim pickings. The real funds would be transferred into the account the island people had set up for that purpose decades ago. They had not come up to talk to the artificials and pass on some of their humanity for what seemed like forever. There was only a stream of information about the originals' lives, but Manoli and the other artificials had to play their part mostly from birth memory.

Manoli was sure something was stopping them from coming to take care of this place, and the artificials. But he did not know how to ask about it. His directives forbade him to talk about it to any outsider and the rest of the artificials knew as much if not less than him.

People changed—ten years was a long time to improvise someone else's life.

Worry was just beginning to creep in Manoli's mind again when he caught a glimpse of the woman on the other side of the glass doors.

Amelia.

He could tell it was her from the calm yet firm way she was arguing with the porter boy over the run-down backpack she always carried. But there were many ways he could have recognized her. Her shape and mannerisms were so familiar to him, that even the databank could never fill in the details quite the same way. She was in her early 50's now, exactly like him. But after all those years she still kept her brown hair in the tightest ponytail that was now swaying left and right.

Manoli shook his head but a smile had crept on his lips. He felt relieved and checked Amelia in before she even came through the doors.

It was when she did come through the glass doors that the

annoying message from the base of his skull informed him: *incoming client.* Manoli clenched his jaw but didn't let it spoil the moment.

Amelia smiled widely as she approached, backpack in hand. Victory. Behind her the youngest porter boy, who also was the youngest artificial, bore a grimace that Manoli placed somewhere between defeat and worry about doing his job right. He was after all only fifteen. And the sadness of it made Manoli forgiving of the boy's mistakes.

'Have I got plans for you this year,' she said upon seeing him. 'Nice to see you again, my friend.' She reached over the counter and squeezed his hand.

For a moment his spinal brain fought with his conscious one. His spinal brain insisted that he give the client her room key right away and take that backpack out of her hands. But his conscious brain, did not want to do any of these. Yet, he was a professional, like human Manoli was before him. So he gave Amelia her room key and turned to the boy who was standing by the corner looking sheepish.

'Good job,' he said with a nod. 'Now, take her bags upstairs.'

Amelia looked on as the boy got inside the elevator. When the doors shut she turned to Manoli with a curious look on her face.

'He is so young! I never see local kids running around these days.'

Thank God for that. This form is not for children, Manoli thought. But he did not say it. His spine would not let him anyway. He was incapable of causing harm to his makers. And that's what would happen if people found out.

'Children would be a distraction to their parents,' he said instead.

There was a strange gleam in her eyes when he said this. Then she looked away and just like that, it was gone.

Manoli left his place behind the counter and joined Amelia. 'I am so glad you are here. How is your family?'

She leaned in and hugged him. Manoli let himself be hugged for a brief moment. It was the fullest of a person he had felt for some time.

The spinal brain stayed silent. They were encouraged to appear human after all, otherwise someone might see behind the illusion. Although it didn't take much to throw tourists off. They almost never cared for a deeper connection.

'So,' he said, after he escaped her affections. 'What have you got for me this year?'

Amelia's eyes shone bright as she looked at him with the expression of her seventeen-year-old self (a face etched in Manoli's birth memory forever) and whispered, 'Butterfly Island.'

*

Butterfly Island was two hours by boat from Santo. It did not belong to the people of the city and therefore had no artificials secretly living there. No humans either. Only butterflies.

Manoli had been to Butterfly Island. But only in his birth memory. That meant that human Manoli had visited the place at least once before the artificial Manoli was born. When he was born, at age seventeen, he had not only the original's personality but many of his memories, especially his fondest ones.

Human Manoli had registered the greenness of the landscape and the butterflies pouring out of every corner of the island. A guide had led them to the most populated part of the forest. Human Manoli had walked up and down the winding stairs, clutching the wooden banisters tightly so he wouldn't trip and fall from gazing at the swarms of Plain Tigers becoming one with the trees or fluttering between human bodies, between his small legs, unfazed.

Those memories were the brightest and the most colorful, even from the ones he made on his own. Manoli could not decide if that was because he was not a real person and so unable to create vivid memories, or because his life was so tinged by his confined existence that everything seemed dull.

*

Early in the morning Manoli dashed down the stone-paved alleyways. For this foray he preferred the least trodden places—if there was anything left truly untrodden on the island. That time of day there weren't many tourists out and about. It was too early for the ones that spent most of their time by the pool, baking under the sun or too late for the ones that returned in the first morning hours after a night of debauchery at the local clubs.

For a few precious hours the island seemed to belong only to the artificials.

Manoli let himself feel enchanted by the walls painted bright summer colors but also by the pure white ones, as radiant as the sun. By the calm sea and the oceanic pools (such was their architecture that they seem to pour into the sea like a tilted glass of water). As he went up the wide and curved stairs that led to a small white church, he admired its decrepit beauty, the chipped green paint of the bells. The priest, another artificial, pulled at the rope and let them boom all the way out to the sea, his long black robes and bushy beard blowing in the high wind. He greeted Manolis with a subtle nod and then crossed his hands and fixed his stare at the horizon.

How could the priest reconcile his nature with his birth memory? Did he still believe he was a God's creature? Manoli wondered the same thing about every artificial but he always reached the same conclusion: it depended on the person they were made from. Their birth memories and the personality their human had. They could not escape it.

Things were bad. Far worse than any other time. Manoli spent most of the morning evaluating damages around the island, trying to find a way to repair what could be repaired. A whole wing in the Heliotrope Hotel had to be closed off just in case the cracks went deeper than they appeared. Then there were the pubs and the restaurants in need of restoration.

Many of those places used to be schools and public buildings but their purpose changed when the wave of tourists increased. Soon the locals could not leave their houses without an official announcement and the hospitals were too full to care both for the locals and the tourists during the summer time. A choice had to be made.

Manoli placed an order for building supplies with the people of the city underneath. He shook his head because he knew they would probably never arrive. It had been like that for a long time now. The standardized supplies would arrive on schedule, those that were arranged many years ago. But anything new or unexpected would be inconsistent or decreased. He would rummage through boxes and crates of supplies for the shops, the restaurants, and the hotels and he would still not find anything useful to rebuild the island. Or maybe, if he were lucky, he would find a fourth of what was needed. Yet, his spine crackled with happiness, rewarding him for his meticulousness.

The way home was long and tedious because it was noon and the tourists were hungry, both for food and local attractions. They poured themselves on the streets like a swarm of locusts cascaded on the crops. *Excuse me* and *I am sorry*, were the two most uttered sentences during the summer, especially during rush hours. They echoed around the island as he made his way between a family of five (already a lobster-red sunburn coating their faces, necks and shoulders).

Manoli tried to make himself small and insignificant as he guessed which streets would be the least busy this time of the day.

He took a sudden turn to the right, to what people usually though was a cul-de-sac even though it wasn't. He did not have to think about it. It was a body memory over the years of navigating the maze of walls. Then he froze. The man who was staring at him had his face by a 92% approximation. And it was a human face. Manoli could tell. The man froze too but only for a few seconds. Then he turned abruptly around, returned to the main street and let the current of tourists carry him away.

*

They sat at the table with the red checkered tablecloth in the tavern's back yard. It was a bad spot, the smells were wafting warm and mist-like from the kitchen and there was nothing to see so close against the wall. But it was quiet and that was good enough for Amelia. So Manoli obliged.

This was supposed to be his day off. Even artificials should appear to have one. That's how he managed to bypass the spine's directives and his spine did not object.

What he could not bypass was the thought of the man on the street.

Manoli ran his face through the databank again and again (the spinal brain was suspiciously silent during his research) but he found nothing. This thought prodded him all day, and if he did not have records of the man, one getting inside a tour bus and another one at the port, from earlier today, he could believe he had imagined it all.

'Ah, but you have to see this.' Amelia nudged Manoli. 'They are literally everywhere!'

The Butterfly Island again.

His friend was not the laid back type. She was not one to take no for an answer either. Manoli had learned that much. Over the years he had accompanied her everywhere around the island. Rock climbing, and wine tasting, and museum tours, and scuba diving. They did everything together. And she kept coming back for almost thirty years with a sort of fierce loyalty for this place. Manoli was afraid to ask why in case she realized it wasn't really worth the trouble after all.

'I will come if you ask me the right way,' Manoli said. A smile parted his lips even though inside he was dead serious.

Amelia would never ask him the right way though. She wouldn't know how. But it wasn't just that. When Manoli thought of the outside world, a feeling like sinking in quicksand washed over him. He was small and the world was too big for the half person he was. It asphyxiated him.

The first time Amelia came back to the island was after her college was over. She was alone, without her parents in the background complaining about their daughter's constant demands to explore.

Manoli had recognized her instantly even thought they had never met before. The fluttering of their first kiss was still fresh on his lips even though it wasn't him who had kissed her. That was the seventeen-year-old human Manoli. The boy had been taken by her. But the memory of that kiss remained always so fresh, so alive. It came back to haunt him in the beginning of every summer. And Manoli was only four years old and soul-crushed because he was aware and he remembered everything, but he was not human Manoli. He was his property.

When Amelia had come straight to him with her wide smile, her eyes shining, he could not resist being her friend. She infused humanity in him in the most unexpected ways. He was the best Manoli he could be just for her. The perfect simulation of him, for thirty years. And she never seemed to notice the difference. Their bond grew stronger.

'Have you ever visited an underwater city?'

The question slipped from his mouth without much thought. The spine punished him for it by creaking loudly inside his head. Manoli shut his eyes dazed. Amelia didn't notice.

'Oh, God no.' A crease burrowed in the skin between her eyebrows. 'They are such claustrophobic places I hear, and so hard to reach. Humans are not meant to live underwater.'

The waiter interrupted when she laid down greaseproof paper and on top of it freshly baked bread, a plate of blood-red tomatoes cut in big chunks and drizzled with olive oil and oregano, fried halloumi, slow-roasted eggplant with feta cheese, sesame and mint pies dipped in honey, and wild leeks in lemon sauce.

Manoli thanked her.

The waiter's eyes fell on him and then on Amelia, and back again as if saying: *What are you doing, brother? This is a dangerous game you are playing.*

'Is this where you want to go?' Amelia bit into one of the pies. The smell of mint spilled all around them. Manoli's spine warned him again. This time with a simple message: *change the subject.*

'No, no.'

'We could try and visit if you'd like to.'

Light flashed inside his eyes. A mild alert for protocol breach.

'Are you okay?' Amelia touched the tip of his fingers; her voice had an edge he could not place.

'I will never leave the island,' he whispered.

Amelia looked at him with her strange gaze again. Sometimes it felt as if she had things to say too but chose not to. Manoli had to remind himself that humans also had secrets. In fact, it was mostly them who had them.

'I can't believe you've never visited Butterfly Island. It's so close,' she said, never taking her eyes off him. 'I really can't believe you've never left this place.'

His skin prickled. If only she stopped pushing him so hard. Maybe if he could tell her the truth she would stop. But then she wouldn't want to be his friend anymore.

'You need to.' Manoli sprang from the chair and ran outside.

He let himself get lost in the crowd until everything was calm.

*

As he was making his way to Heliotrope thinking of all the ways he could apologize and make up to Amelia (for freaking out and leaving her, for not following her to Butterfly Island, for being the copy of someone instead of that someone), he saw that the pool bar's lights were open and soft music was playing in the background.

The bar always gave him a nostalgic feel. It was built to be reminiscent of the island's golden age, slow music, pale yellow lights and idols half-lost in the sands of time. The lack of renovations made the nostalgia almost tangible.

This was not right. The bar should not have opened until later tonight. Manoli ran this inconsistency through the system but found nothing. He paused when he spotted Panos's bus parked outside the hotel's side entrance.

The bus was empty and dark, the door was shut but Manoli could see Panos's figure sitting at the driver's seat. He waived at him but got no response. Perhaps Panos was pretending not to have seen him so he could sneak some more pennies in his jug. He drew closer. Panos did hold the jug between his stubby fingers but he was not doing anything. He seemed lost. His expression was cold. Manoli banged at the door until Panos finally opened.

'What's wrong?' he asked as he got in.

His friend did not reply immediately. When he did reply, it seemed like it took up all of his energy. 'It's over,' he said in one breath. He hugged the jug closer, like a baby.

'What's over?' Manoli remembered the bus from his records. Things suddenly fell into place.

'Where is he?'

Panos's gaze turned to the bar. Manoli saw the solitary

silhouette crouching on a stool. He got off the bus. Panos didn't bother to close the doors behind him.

Manoli felt his throat dry but he kept going, feeling like a man doomed. By what, he would soon find out.

The man was Manoli. The real deal. He was noticeably thinner than artificial Manoli and he sat on the very far corner of the bar, deflated.

When he saw Manoli at the entrance he said, 'Oh, you are here.'

'It's nice to see you again,' Manoli said, numbly.

The human Manoli patted his forehead with a handkerchief.

'The island, my God, I had forgotten how beautiful it is,' he said. His eyes looked sad under the pale lights of the ceiling.

Manoli wore an apathetic expression but inside he was studying the human Manoli, the tone of his voice, his mannerisms. It had been so long since seeing the man up close. His voice had lowered an octave. It had become coarser too. The wrinkles around his sunken eyes had fanned out in a different pattern than he had expected.

His spine, out of habit, made a note to correct those deviations. But he sensed this might not be necessary.

'It's falling apart now,' Manoli said. He tried to make his voice neutral, without judgment. It was too damn hard.

'We shouldn't have left it to you,' human Manoli said, bitterly. He drew the handkerchief to his cheeks and wiped a few lingering drops of sweat. 'We shouldn't have left.'

Manoli felt his anger boiling underneath his skin and no cryostorage could cool it enough. Deeper still, his spine buzzed with something like a warning.

He walked behind the bar just to give himself something to do.

'Would you like something to drink?'

'Tom Collins, please,' said human Manoli, visibly relieved for the pause. 'Thank you.'

Tom Collins sounded about right. It was Manoli's choice of drink as well. He grabbed the best brand of gin from the top shelf and a tall glass and his spine hummed in agreement.

'This last earthquake was very bad. It made us hasten our plans.' Human Manoli sounded small now, almost apologetic.

'Plans?'

Manoli felt the bitter cold of the ice cubes against his fingers. This was how his skin would be carried away to some decomposition and recycling facility. Some place shady, so no one would notice. He eyed the knife.

'Are you planning to kill us?' He tried to move his hand and take the knife from the counter, but the spine wouldn't let him. Both of his arms were dead on his sides. *I just want to slice an orange*, he though. *Just an orange.*

'We plan to take our lives back.'

The spine relented and let him pick up the knife. He cut a slice of orange, thin as rice paper, and finished the drink. Humans had a funny way to describe things. Nobody took their lives from them. They gave them up willingly.

He passed human Manoli the glass.

'Have you got any idea what's like to live down there?' The man's hands were shaking. Some of the drink spilled on the countertop.

Alcohol stains, said Manoli's spine, prodding him to clean it.

'People become apathetic or unruly,' continued human Manoli. 'But most of all they become less like people. It's not worth it anymore.'

'You are killing us,' Manoli whispered.

Alcohol stains, the spine repeated. Manoli put down the knife and grabbed a kitchen wipe. He wiped the stains clean with a ferociousness that scared him.

He felt small, reduced to an object. He wasn't himself anymore but human Manoli's arm or leg, something less than.

'What should I do?' Manoli asked, lost.

'Wait until the summer ends and make sure everyone is underground. We'll take over from there.' Human Manoli's face was red, flushed, as if he was ashamed about what he was about to say. 'Don't bother with the winter staff. They are already done.'

'Done?'

Human Manoli didn't meet his gaze, he just dabbed at his

sweaty face again. Manoli was trying to communicate silently with the winter pods but there was nothing there.

He felt sick. His mind raced to Panos and the other artificials, the fifteen-year-old boy who had barely lived. And finally Amelia.

Summer would never begin with her face again.

Summer would never begin again.

If it weren't for the spine keeping him straight up he would have folded into himself like crumpled paper.

'I know you Manoli,' his human self squeezed his shoulder. It felt like claws against his skin. 'You are like me. A professional.'

'Here you are!'

When Amelia crossed the threshold both of them froze. Manoli thought they looked like shut-down replicants. Almost identical.

Amelia crossed the space between the edge of the pool and the stool next to the one human Manoli was sitting and sat there. She looked over her shoulder at the man sitting next to her. Time seemed to slow down. Manoli searched for a hint of understanding hidden in her eyes, but he could not read her face.

Human Manoli took a couple of bills out of his back pocket and put them on the counter.

'Thanks,' he mumbled. He left as if he was been chased.

Manoli looked down at the bills. They were the expired kind.

'Who was that guy?' Amelia asked. She picked up a paper straw and started chewing away at it. 'He was acting strange.'

'You mean you've never seen him before?'

She shrugged. 'Not that I remember.'

An odd feeling prickled his skin, as if the husk of another person was peeling away and he was underneath it. Someone clear and sharp. Someone with a purpose. He exhaled.

'Hey, listen,' Amelia said, sheepishly. 'I am sorry if I pushed you too hard.'

Manoli took her hand in his and tried to convince both of them when he said, 'I am coming with you.'

*

Manoli looked at the ferry as if this was the first time he saw one. And in a way it was. This ferry was a real thing now. Unlike the usual shadows of ships wafting in the background while he stayed behind, this was a solid three dimensional ship. And he would try to get on it.

'Are you coming or what?'

Amelia lingered on the ferry's gangway a few steps in. She wore a white brimmed hat that hid most of her face under a shadow. Manoli from inside the bus could not tell if she was anxious or just bored. She wore her backpack over her right shoulder. It looked heavier than usual because she was resting it against the railing.

There were other artificials at the dock, mostly bus drivers and porters. They ran around in a frenzy hauling luggage and helping tourists orient themselves.

'This is stupidity,' Panos croaked. Then he hugged Manoli. His face was pressed on Manoli's shoulder so hard it bruised his artificial skin.

'Pure, human stupidity,' he went on. Still, he opened the bus doors and let Manoli get off, the penny-jug wedged tightly between Manoli's arm and torso. A farewell gift.

'We *are* humans,' Manoli said. But Panos was already speeding away from him. He intended to enjoy his last summer alive as best as he could.

Manoli squeezed the jug under his arm a little harder and walked to the gangway.

He reached the edge of the gangway fast. Too fast. Before his courage gave in, his spine reached him right on time. Just like that, he was frozen. Arms and legs fixed, immovable, like a statue made of steel. His spine cracked vengefully, the pain would have made him scream if he could make a sound.

Access to the ferry denied.

He felt the eyes of the artificials pinned on him. Some of them helped carry luggage all the way to the ships. But when their services were not needed anymore they would return to the island without a moment's delay. They did not choose to return of course. They had to. Their existence was not to be revealed to the outside world so the people of the city could return and take everything back as if they were nothing.

'Hurry up,' Amelia said. Then nothing. She did not even move an inch. Manoli sensed she was holding her breath.

Manoli looked at his feet, then at the sea and the horizon beyond, back at Amelia, and at his feet again. His was helpless. He had to turn around and leave her there.

Plain stupidity, he thought.

'Hurry up,' she said again. 'I...I can't carry this all the way up.'

Manoli looked at her. Her face was not a shadow anymore. It was plain and clear and she was looking at him in the eyes.

Then she said, 'Help me, please.'

Manoli's eyes grew bigger. Something was happening. A change. It felt like a distant echo, a non-memory that had somehow etched itself in his software. His spine finally shut up.

This was what calm felt like. He took a few cautious steps on the gangway. Amelia's eyes were misty as she gave him the backpack.

'I'll take this,' he said.

Help me. Help me. She kept saying it until they were on the ferry. *Help me*, until the gangway was lifted. *Help me*, until the engines started. *Help me*, until the faces of the artificial at the dock were the size of a pin. But their eyes were still following him from afar.

It was a fail-safe in the system. He could not leave the island except for when he must. For when a human needed help. Maybe something would happen at sea or an earthquake would eventually prove to be catastrophic. He needed to be able to bring the humans to safety. They mattered and he did not.

This would not last for long, of course. There was a good chance he would not make it to Butterfly Island. When the tracking system would catch up to his position and verify there was no actual threat, bad things would happen. Maybe his spinal brain would shut him down and render him lifeless. Perhaps some safety net would start to erase his mind, so no documents of his existence could be found.

But he still had this body, this steel skeleton and the bioengineered skin. This was proof enough perhaps. And he was already on a ship with Amelia. She would know what to do with him once they were far enough. He trusted her even though he had all the questions in the world for her to answer. But he said nothing for fear that his spine would wake up again.

'Can you talk now?' Amelia was at his side. She lifted her hat and her hair swirled in the sea breeze. It was the first time he had seen her hair like this.

'About what?' He smiled and this time his smile was unbidden.

Amelia nodded and looked at the horizon.

'See?' She pointed at the green shapeless mass on the water. 'This is where we're going.'

Manoli fixed his eyes on that blurry spot between the sea foam and the sky. He was already feeling the memory of this moment forming in his mind, fresh and vivid. Putting his birth memory to shame.

Abacos
Lina Theodorou

Translators from Greek: Dimitra Nikolaidou, Vaya Pseftaki

2:15 p.m., family lunch: You've never moved from your workspace.
Formulation 456: Today, I want to get drunk.
Code 376: Easter at the village, special offer including a ten-day fast complete with fresh vegetables at half the price.

Journalist: While at first considered the ultimate threat to the market, in the end Abacos technology has only altered the market's form. And to think, all that began as an innovative treatment for alcoholism, correct?

Abacos Representative: Correct, but it wasn't just that. For a long time, vegetarian products were mimetic. You bought meatless ham, steaks made out of enriched linseed. For a product to win the market over, a specific branding was required. Entirely synthetic food had not met with much success either; it tasted bland, and its effect on people's health was suspect.

J: For a very long time, gastronomic free choice movements were breaking down in fierce interfaction conflicts. Things happened simultaneously: on one hand we had global shortages, and on the other, new discoveries about the brain's chemical structure.

AR: Abundance, as a by-product of prosperity, in every respect constitutes an important value of human civilization, and yes, the truth is that nobody lacks anything anymore. It's just a matter of the right dosage. Besides, what's left is either not natural, or belongs to a museum. But even if this wasn't the case, who has the stomach or the teeth to consume it nowadays?

J: Do you have anything to say to those who protest, in no small numbers, that most formulations remain far too expensive?

AR: I'm going to be honest with you. Prices fluctuate widely, but there is also a great variety of products that everyone can afford. This is not the case though for face creams or services. Look at the advantages, however: there are no shortages as far as it concerns our cultures or special preferences, since everything is at our disposal. Drinking formulations still remain the most popular, but there are also injections, plasters, suppositories and so on.

J: You were initially accused of replacing the farmers' market and the super markets with drugstores.

AR: There is an objective difference, but the experience remains exactly the same. The only thing you need to do, is consume the right formulation at the right place. From the beginning, the determining factor that led to the rapid spread of Abacos food technology was the extremely easy installation and activation of the device whose physical existence is necessary, in order for the body to interact with the food formula.

J: Tell us a few words on how you dealt with the problem of overconsumption.

AR: In case of alcohol, the liver is not affected, perceptual experience remains the same, and most importantly, there are no aftereffects.

J: Still, someone could choose to be constantly intoxicated.

AR: The price of the product itself would function as a preventative. We also applied further safety valves in the product coding, something we could not do with actual alcohol. There is an upper weekly tolerance limit, and even in cases of extreme consumption, the effects are greatly reduced or even made minimal. The same strategy was employed in cases of food over-consumption.

J: How do you deal with the illegal products that inevitably came out, having of course violated these safety valves?

AR: Yes, this is still happening, but with the introduction of stricter laws, the percentage of offenders has dropped significantly. This might also be due to the fact that formulations always take effect with the help of the equivalent devices located in real space, while without them they just cover your biological needs, like a form of compressed astronaut food. At home or at a restaurant, in open or closed spaces, it is relatively difficult to surpass the initial limit of the experience on offer. On the other hand of course, there are also the illegal venues…

J: Still, a lot of people are not thrilled with the idea of going to a restaurant where no one cooks.

AR: Basically, not much has changed. Everyone takes part in the process, with the main difference being that there is no raw material involved. Technology keeps advancing, all data concerning food or the virtual space where we can enjoy it are registered, and they continue to combine with each other. No jobs were lost, on the contrary, thousands of new ones were created, and mind you, constructing gastronomic experiences is not an easy task.

J: How do you explain that even though Abacos technology first spread due to food shortages, it quickly evolved into a new form of art?

AR: The Mediterranean always had a rich culinary tradition. Even though at first it seemed that it would be far more difficult for Abacos technology to spread here without an uproar, eventually, due to our past, our high aesthetics and our culture, we became pioneers in the field. The high status of the Greek chefs is telling, especially when compared to their foreign colleagues— they almost monopolize laboratory positions.

J: Our past experience in the tourist industry certainly played a role in that. Apart from the good climate and the sea, one of the main attractions of Greece has always been the exquisite food. But lately, we've lost those little taverns, among others…

AR: We lost those, and yet we didn't. Now that we are capable of shaping the virtual environment, no one misses the tavern even if they are in Siberia. The simulation is so versatile, that the experience doesn't even have to be a lonely one, since it can be shaped according to the social environment as well. No one deprives you of the joy of eating with company.

Isn't it for example amazing that we, having taken the formulation 3487, are able to enjoy two cappuccinos plus two delicious pieces of chocolate cake in this very atmospheric coffee shop, while none of this has ever happened and we're actually sitting on a bench in Karytsi square? Yet, in our minds all of it is real, nothing's missing. Caffeine's already given us a boost, while sugar does zero damage to our blood vessels—though today, we might've splurged a bit in our search for the best quality possible…

Any Old Disease
Dimitra Nikolaidou

'What is *wrong* with him?'

Ada had heard that tone before, the horror of a newly assigned doctor witnessing the Leak for the first time. She waited for the novice's breath to settle.

'He is withering,' she said, her gaze fixed upon the man slowly expiring in front of them, his eyes already blinded, his skin paper-thin and stained. 'For years on end, he is going to waste away; his remaining senses will dull, his organs will fail and in the end, he will die. This is what doctors here refer to as the Leak. As for what exactly is wrong with him, what the causes are and how it can be stopped—well, this is exactly what we are trying to figure out here, in this Institute. This is why we need you.' She let that sink in. This was the make-or-break moment, when someone decided whether they had the stomach to stay and deal with the horror on a daily basis, or walked away and drank themselves to oblivion.

The younger woman crossed her arms in front of her, eyes still fixed on the man beyond the glass. So far, she seemed to take it in better than Ada herself had, so many years ago.

'I will do everything I can to find a cure for this disease,' the woman said in the end, and Ada let go of a breath she had not realized she was holding. She had liked this one from the start; it would have been a pity to see her go the way of so many others.

*

The novice's name was Cybele and now that she had made up her mind to stay, Ada could finally allow herself to get to know her. The two of them rode the glass elevator that went all the way up to the Institute's terrace in silence, emerging as the sun's last rays bled over the snow-covered mountains.

The view was sublime as always, yet it failed to draw a reaction out of the Cybele; she kept staring at her drink instead.

'It gets better,' Ada said, after a few moments of silence.

Cybele glanced at her, lips parted, and then turned back to her cup. The signs of shock were still etched on her face; the sun-tanned skin was now cast in grey, and her green eyes, so bright and curious this morning, had retreated into their sockets.

Ada said no more, let the woman compose her thoughts in peace. To see patients dying of the Leak took the wind out of your lungs; it was not so much the physical decay, the so very slowly crumbling skin, the hair turning to ash. No disease was a pleasant sight, after all. No, there was something else about the Leak, something visceral, whispering threats under your skin, pulling you when common sense told you to run. But then again, common sense was not the strong suit of anyone working at the Institute.

'I apologize.' Cybele said eventually. 'I thought I was prepared.'

'This isn't any old disease. It has that effect on everyone who encounters it. Take your time.'

Cybele nodded. Her eyes seemed to take in the landscape around them before settling back on Ada.

'Do they understand what's happening to them?'

'They understand everything at first. Yet by the end, even the mind is gone.' Some considered this a blessing. Ada did not.

'Why is this disease so little known outside the Institute?' Cybele asked. 'I tried to read up on it before coming up here but there's very little out there. Just a few vague footnotes, and an ancient, inconclusive case study.'

Ada shrugged. 'Well, this is the rarest of diseases. No known cause, no cure. Every single case is brought to us, and since we still do not know how it spreads, we have chosen to remain as isolated as we can. Plus, for now, we do not want to publish our findings.'

'Why not?'

'Institute's policy. As obscure as a black cat's soul.'

For the first time after witnessing the Leak, Cybele's eyes came back to focus. 'But then, where do the Institute's funds come from? This facility looks anything but cheap.'

Ada lifted the cup to her lips. 'The Director scored us a government contract, untold eons ago. It means we're under the Health Ministry's thumb, but it's a relief to actually work instead of hunting down funds every second semester.'

Cybele did not speak for a moment, then mimicked Ada's shrug. She settled on her chair a little better. 'And this?' she asked, looking at Ada's glossy chrome and matte carbon-fiber left hand. 'Did you get it working here?'

'This? No... no.' Ada clenched the metal fingers, then left them immobile again. 'It was a landmine in New Paris.' She held the hand up and the fingers caught the last flashes of the setting sun, silver painted molten red. 'I can't be a surgeon anymore of course, but it beats a pirate's hook.'

Cybele laughed, and Ada smiled back. The memory always summoned pinpricks of fire on her skin, but she sensed the unspoken questions in the air and pressed on.

'We were a bunch of volunteers from the medical faculty, searching for survivors in the ruins. We had gone as far as the Louvre crater, and were looking for a way to pass through when our guide slipped and landed face down on the wrong side of a minefield.'

This was as much as she could say for now—perhaps in a few hundred years she would be able to talk about the rest, about flying deafened through the debris and the flame, about landing on her best friend's body, about Milo and Anwuli pulling her away seconds before the collapse, or about or any of the things that came after. For the time being, she just took another gulp.

'Prosthetics are the reason I decided to go into medicine,' Cybele said, shifting the subject. Empathy; a useful trait in a doctor. 'Everyone else thought I was destined to be a historian, or a journalist. Something with digging up the past, anyway. The world had 10 billion people before the Great Floods, and all their stories are now lost; someone has to find them, and I wanted it to be me. However, in the end I found myself so touched by the engineering feats of prosthetists, that I knew I had to be a part of it.'

'Prosthetics don't do anything for them, you know,' Ada said, nodding towards the underground labs where the Leak drained their patients away. 'Nothing does.'

'And they just wither away like that? Till they are gone?'

Ada nodded. 'You will get attached to your first. I won't say don't do it; we all did.'

Cybele didn't answer. She took another sip, lips tight, fingers tense. She seemed secretive, but it mattered little. Isolated as they were up in the mountain, miles away from any village, everyone opened up eventually, and let go.

After all, they had all the time in the world.

*

The Institute was a pile of glass boxes, panels, and domes, designed to let as much light as possible slip in through the day. The Leaks, however, were secured underground; they were too fragile, and always cold. As a result, Ada had to spend half her day below the frozen earth with them and at the end of her every shift, no matter how sharp the alpine cold was, she always needed to go outside the crystal walls even for a minute, in order to start breathing again.

'How is the novice doing?'

Milo asked the question as soon as the elevator started moving towards the terrace. In the six months that had passed since she and Cybele had shared their first coffee up there, the days had become much shorter. The sun had already set when they stepped out, but the view remained magnificent; starlight reflected on sculpted snow.

'Better than most,' Ada said. The elevator doors closed behind them without a sound and they both let a few moments pass, bathing in the night. So far up the mountains there was almost no wildlife to break the silence—just their own long exhalations, carrying away the day. 'She caught up fast, doesn't flinch near the Leaks, even asked a couple of questions that got me thinking.'

Milo let a half-laugh out. 'Doesn't flinch? Are you sure she's human?'

'Shut up.' She just looked at the snow for a moment, half a word riding on each breath but none getting out of her lips. 'I wish I knew how she does it. It is getting in the way of our research, the way the disease freaks out the rest of us.'

'I know. I know.' Levity had been chased away from his tone now. 'Hey, if she can do what we can't, we are lucky to have her here. Just... don't blame yourself for not being her.'

Her anger evaporated and she sighed. 'I know. She just reminded me why I signed up for this in the first place. She cares for them the way I used to care when I first came here – nowadays, I feel I'm just continuing the work out of stubbornness.'

'It takes all kinds. The compassionate, the stubborn, the morbidly fascinated and even those of us trapped up here by our bloody contract.' He closed his eyes and stretched, head to toe. 'Not that I do not share your frustration. Sometimes, for all our hard work, I swear we are just going in circles.'

'True.' They weren't supposed to talk about work after their shift had ended; eight hours with the Leaks were draining enough. Some days, though, were more intense than others and today, their oldest patient had refused to continue treatment. It would be a matter of days before her clouded eyes closed out the world for good –her life seeping towards the darkness in the center of the earth.

The words snuck out of Ada's mouth. 'What if... what if we aren't meant to find the truth?'

'What?'

'Come on. We've circled the issue before, let us say it out loud. There are files missing from the Institute's research. You can tell by the serial numbers. Most of it is older work, but still. Why lock away anything at all, if we're so desperate for answers?'

Milo looked at her. For a moment, the stars did not blink.

'Are you the one who put Cybele up to it, then?' he asked.

'Up to what?'

'Snooping. Asking to cross-reference old research. Was it you?'

'What? Of course not. When did that happen? And why

would I set a newcomer to do my snooping for me? I've been here forever.'

'I'm sorry.' He ran his hand through his hair. 'You've wondered aloud about the missing files so many times in the past, and the Director never reacts well to the implication, so...'

She waited, but Milo had stopped talking. 'So you thought I conned the rookie into asking on my behalf,' she said, arms crossed.

'Hey, I would've done it if I were you. Anything to avoid his stare. Noticed how he started locking his office door a month ago? How he revoked half our access codes for no reason? I think he hired extra guards a week ago; some of the faces outside the fence are new. He's getting more paranoid by the day.'

Ada had noticed, but she was still pissed at Milo, and chose to leave all his words unanswered.

*

Three months after that spat, spring rode over the mountain top. Now the third floor cafeteria was always full early in the mornings; nobody wanted to lose a moment of sunlight before heading underground to work. She braced herself for the cheerfulness, but the minute she walked in, everyone stopped talking for the briefest of moments, and then resumed chattering with half an eye turned towards her.

Milo was the only one to keep his eyes on her; she moved towards his table, but then he nodded imperceptibly towards the windows. With one last glance at him, she walked up to the glass, and looked outside.

The sun was melting the scarce snow they had gotten last night, and Cybele was out there, holding the last flakes in her hands. Showing them to a Leak.

Ada sighed on the inside. The new ones always got attached, and then did something stupid about it. The Leaks—*the patients*—were exactly as fragile as they looked. Taking them out of the underground bunker was not doing them any favors. This one seemed so far down the road, that even talking in the chilly air burdened his lungs. On the other hand, they all had done something like that when they were as fresh as Cybele was. Ada would have a talk with her later on.

Ada turned away, only to find herself almost stepping on the Director's toes.

It took her a few more seconds to realize that the cafeteria had fallen silent, everyone staring in their cups, ears cocked to her side.

'Look at her,' the Director said, through a mirthless smile. He was a head taller than her, and made of slippery ice. 'Brave, isn't she?'

Ada did not answer. Cybele looked up. The Director did not acknowledge her; he brought his cup to his lips but did not drink. Cybele turned to her patient again, as if he were the only person in the world.

Around them, snow began falling again.

*

'How do you do this?'

'Do what?' Cybele was several steps ahead as they climbed down the snow-dusted slope, but she stopped and turned.

'Be so comfortable around them.' Cybele remained silent, and eventually Ada caught up to her. They stared at the distance for a while. Below them, whiffs of clouds concealed the valley at the feet of the mountains. The pyramidal tip of an old church steeple, probably buried under the ground three thousand years ago, when the Great Floods had covered the old world in water, was the only landmark as far as their eyes could see.

'I don't know,' Cybele said at the end. 'Why not? In the end, it is just another disease. You get used to the symptoms and proceed to the treatment.'

'I know. But for most of us, it took much, much longer.'

'So everyone keeps telling me. Sometimes, I think I freak you out as much as the patients do.'

'True,' Ada said. Cybele looked up at her in surprise; the older woman simply shrugged. It took a few more seconds before they both burst out laughing. 'You do score points for constantly aggravating the Director, however.'

'Not my intention,' said Cybele, and her tone made Ada hold her next words back. Just mentioning the man's name seemed to cast a shadow these days, and the mountain light was receding too fast for comfort anyway.

'So where are you from? I never asked,' she said instead, kicking a stone down the slope. It did not even echo as it rolled.

'Northern Greece. The great wind farms. Ever been there?'

'No. Not yet. Perhaps when I am done with the Institute.'

'You have a bucket list for afterwards?'

'Not really. Who knows what I will want to do when I'm finished here. Probably just fish in the sun for the next thirty years. Not that my contract expires any time soon.'

'Has anyone ever left?'

Ada hesitated. It sounded too sinister to say it out loud that no, nobody ever had. There was work to be done, still, and after so long, the outside seemed distant and noisy. Cybele stared at her a few seconds more, and then turned back to look at the setting sun being impaled on the solitary church steeple.

'Come on, let's walk a bit more' she said. 'We don't have much time left.'

*

Shots woke Ada up in the night.

Her eyes opened. She should be startled, should maybe even panic as the dry sounds tore the air. As she reached for the light, though, she realized she had been half-waiting for something big to happen, ever since Cybele had taken the patient out in the snow half a year ago. When you live so long in a place, you can read the change in the air.

There was no alarm going off, no red lights blinking. If she hadn't heard shots before, she might even write the sound off as a distant avalanche and go back to sleep. However, this was not a choice now. She got up, found her morning clothes and slipped her white coat over them—the most useless armor ever.

She cracked her door open and looked across the corridor, at Cybele's room.

The door was half open, and no-one was inside. No laptop on the desk either.

She was preparing to go over when an armed man in black uniform turned the corner. Her heart clenched; the Institute guards did not carry weapons and they had never stepped inside the main building, for as long as she had worked there. This man was military; an outsider.

'Are you all right, Doctor?' he asked, cold in his tracks.

'What is going on?'

'You are not to worry. Please return to your room.'

'I need to check on my patients.' Cybele was closer to them than to her colleagues; perhaps Ada would find some kind of answer in their quarters. The man was not actively stopping her, but there is a thing about guns, they talk in a way mouths can't. 'Getting them upset is not good, for any one.'

Yes, he had his guns—but she could always rely on the terrifying aura of the Leak.

It worked. 'All right, Doctor. You can go down, but I will need to escort you.'

She nodded and walked to the underground entrance, the guard one step behind her, his boots leaving muddied prints on the pristine floor. She had hoped to get rid of him once they reached the basement but of course, no such luck. The accordion doors parted for them, and they entered the underground.

He gasped at the sight of the Leaks behind the glass walls; his sudden shock would be her only chance. She ducked into one of the glass rooms fast, and closed the door before he could gather up the courage to follow. It locked behind her, and she hoped the man would not know how much she was going against the rules by doing this.

She knelt by the bed, and whispered to the patient under the covers. 'I'm Cybele's friend. I need to help her. Please, if you do know, tell me what's going on. Is she safe?'

The man was one of their oldest patients; his hair had fallen off long ago and his skin was stained, crumpled paper. He wasn't sleeping; the Leak took their sleep away after a while. Twisted fingers held the covers close to the chest. They were always cold after this stage, no matter the temperature.

She caught herself bending forward, trying to inhale the crumpled skin. The disease beckoned as it always did, and it took all her experience and training to resist. Her fingers touched the covers, twitched as she tried not to touch the patient himself.

'Did she make it out?' the man asked. Their voice was the worst, the disharmony in it. It echoed out of a grave and forced you to come closer, to listen.

'Cybele?' she whispered. The man looked at her. 'I'm not sure. I'm her friend, though. Do you know where she is?'

'I know you. I saw you watching us over the deck so many months ago, when she showed me the snowflakes.'

She did not answer. His labored breath ticked the seconds off.

'She liked to visit the black church,' he said. 'She liked to watch the sun rise from there.'

Ada waited some more, but the man only exhaled. It wore them out, talking, much as they craved it. And much as she craved an answer, the pull was becoming too much. She stood up and walked out, smoothing her jacket all the way down.

Outside, the soldier was holding on to his gun. He was fighting hard not to vomit, but for the first time in her life, Ada could not conjure any sympathy at all.

'Is he... is he...?'

'Going to be all right? What do you think?' she answered, walking past him and reaching for the stairs.

'And he was born like that?'

It caught up with her, then, compassion. She slowed down, took a breath. 'It's a very rare disease, sir. You shouldn't worry— it affects less than one person in ten million. I suggest visiting Dr. Kira here, first thing in the morning. Talk about it. She will help you get it out of your mind.'

Her concern shamed him back into stony silence, and they walked out.

*

Next morning at breakfast, the usual cliques had merged into one big, animated hydra. Ada was expecting them to be awkward with her as she walked in, cup in hand, but they had all been together for too long; after a second, they circled her, eyes gleaming.

'Have you heard?'

'I only heard the gunshots.' They did not believe her; they waited for more. 'All right. Anyone care to shock me with the terrible news?'

Milo stepped forward, steaming cup in hand. 'Cybele is nowhere to be found. Haven't the guards come to question you yet?'

Question her—odd choice of words.

'Cybele ran off?' She could feel her heart skipping beats, but would not give them the satisfaction. 'And why the fuss? She wouldn't be the first to break down in here.'

'She did not break down. Or run off. She broke into the Director's office. Using very precise, very professional methods.'

She looked at them startled, and they looked back, waiting.

'Did she take anything?'

'He won't tell of course,' said Milo. 'But she must have. They caught her down the slope, halfway to the river. I heard there was a boat waiting for her there but whoever drove it escaped when the guards grabbed her.'

'Where is she now?'

'A government helicopter came for her at sunrise.'

'You said government?'

The crack in her voice shut them up. Leaving her cup on the table, she walked outside and, thank their oaths, her colleagues found it in themselves to respect that and leave her alone, till the soldiers came in her room to ask her their empty questions.

*

'Still thinking about her?'

'You can tell?'

Six months had passed since Cybele was taken away, but Milo knew Ada well enough.

'At least the Director isn't looking at you funny anymore.'

'Why would he? He's the one who hired her. And it was his decision to appoint Cybele to me in the first place. It's not like I had anything to do with her schemes.'

Milo nodded and laid back. The time had not come yet for a frank discussion, and they both knew it.

Ada got up. 'Going for a walk,' she said. 'Last days of summer.'

He raised his cup, and she smiled, buttoned up her coat and walked out of the glass doors. She had been taking walks every day for the past five months, till the guards had eventually stopped tailing her and everyone had started taking her new habit for granted. Only today, instead of going towards the summit, she turned around, and went the way she had been long avoiding, the path down the slope.

The path towards the 'black church'.

It wasn't a church anymore, of course. Ages ago, it might have been the roof of one, probably considered ancient even before the Great Floods swept the old world away. The rest of the building had been submerged in mud but the top, built to withstand hail and stone, had remained, jutting out of the earth, catching the light on its dark tiles.

It took some searching but finally she noticed it, the place where the moss had been disturbed. She knelt and slid her artificial hand over it. The whole tile dislodged and a dew-covered tin caught the sunrays. There was a box there—Cybele's lunch box.

It opened easily under the pressure of her metal fingers, and Ada saw two things inside; a musty book that looked as old as the sunken church itself, and a digital data stick. She picked the tome first and slid her fingers in the old pages, trying not to inhale their rotten scent. The handwriting was hard to read, but she could tell it was some kind of ledger, a list of births and deaths in the small village that used to lie half a mile below, long before the Floods had taken it with them three millennia ago.

Only there was something wrong with the events recorded inside. First of all, it seemed that everyone who had ever been born in that village, had eventually died. Not only that, they had also died very young: at seventy, at eighty, some of them even at sixty. The most peculiar thing, though, was that the archivist had labeled all those premature deaths as 'natural causes.'

It made no sense.

'I am impressed.' The Director's voice, just a few steps behind.

A split second; her sole chance. She dropped the box and as she scrambled to pick it up, she stepped on the data stick and pushed it into the mud.

She turned around and there he was, looking at her, hands behind his back. No armed guards, she noticed. She exhaled, and looked at him; he extended his hand and she handed the book over without shutting it, trying to get a last glimpse at the handwritten litany of death.

For a moment they stood in silence, he reading, and she pushing the stick further into the ground.

'I am sorry for your friend,' he said eventually, startling her. His own eyes had not widened as he looked over the ledger. 'Had she told you of this?'

'No. I figured it out a few days ago,' she half-lied. 'Pieced some of the things she had implied together. I wanted to see if I was right.'

She could see he did not believe her, and she decided to go all in.

'What does it mean, though?' she asked. 'What killed this people? Why natural causes? What happened in this mountain?'

'No idea, Doctor,' he smiled through his teeth. 'I will study this and let you know when I understand myself.'

He turned his back and left, and Ada wanted to knock him over for a moment but then she noticed his shoulders hunching and his steps growing heavy as he walked away. Kneeling to clean her boots, she picked the data stick up.

*

Security had tightened since Cybele's stunt, but the guard in the gate was used to Ada's artificial hand setting off the alarm; they did not notice the stick tucked inside the glove, chrome on chrome. Back to her room, she sealed the windows, took her tablet to the bathroom, sat on the edge of the bathtub and slid the stick in.

Only one folder inside, untitled. No notes, no documents, only photos: underwater graveyards, larger than anything she had ever seen, and extremely short lifespans carved on each one. Seventy years. Sixty. Forty. Some of them had pictures enshrined in them, and she could see that most of the deceased had fallen victims to the Leak before their deaths: the lined faces, the cloudy eyes, the false teeth.

This made no sense. She was no historian, and even if she were, there was precious little left from the world before the floods. However, even though the waters and the wars that followed had obliterated written records, just as they had swept away everything else, some stories had been recorded a few decades after the disaster, once the few survivors stopped fighting and scraping for food, settled down and started to rebuild over the ruins. They spoke of famine, and salted earth and the fires that broke out in the abandoned cities, consuming what was left. They spoke of the Himalayan ice melting, flooding the world a second time, prolonging their struggle. They spoke of the diseases they had to combat without access to hospitals or medicine, the wounds that took decades to heal, their cancers that had to wait a hundred years for previously known cures to be re-invented. Yet there was no mention of a Leaking epidemic in their scarce tellings, no word of people simply wasting away with time till they were dead.

A knock on her room's door. Oh well. It had taken him long enough.

She got up, opened the bathroom door, crossed the sitting room. The Director was on the outside. Again, no armed guards with him. He inclined his head, and she stepped back to let him in. The door closed behind him.

'So, you really did not know,' he pointed out. 'I apologize for the bluff. I had to make sure you were not allied with them.'

'Them?'

'The Pures. Cybele's little terrorist group.' She kept staring at him, and he sighed. 'Can I have the data stick, or whatever it was? You would not have given me the book so easily, if you weren't holding on to something else.'

'Of course. Can I have an explanation in return? I've been working on the Leak for the last two hundred and seventy-five years. Milo was here a century before me. This,' she pointed at the tablet, still sitting on the bathroom sink, 'looks like something we should've known.'

'I know. I apologize, Doctor; I did not enjoy keeping secrets myself, but the position of the Director came with caveats.'

'Yet you let me find it. You could've stopped me before I reached the church.'

'Again, I do not enjoy keeping secrets, even as I understand the need for them. They are the death of science.' He leaned on her wall, arms crossed. 'Speaking of secrets, by now you might have realized how your protégé had us all fooled. I invited her over after encountering her impressive research on prosthetics and regenerative techniques. And at first, she seemed the most dedicated of all of us. Yet it seems, she never meant to heal the Leak.'

'Oh? Then what was she doing up here? The view isn't that magnificent.'

He did not crack a smile. 'I believe she meant to sneak one of the patients out, or at least secure samples and photos, and spread them into the general population.' He paused for a moment, glancing at her, then went on. 'You see, the Pures believe the disease and its conclusion, death, to be our natural state—something to strive for, instead of a horrible illness. Which is why Cybele wormed her way up here, so she could find a way to spread the word and, maybe, the disease itself.' He scrutinized her face for a moment. 'This is the first time you are hearing of that.'

'It is.' Cybele, as she knew her, was shredded; she would pick the pieces later, rebuild a new Cybele. Out of the maelstrom though, one thing remained. 'She did make you wonder, didn't she? You did ponder, could she possibly be right?'

He smiled a tight smile. 'Perhaps? Doesn't the sight of the Leak strike a chord a bit too deep for comfort? What other disease does that to us, after so long?' He stopped leaning on the wall, and took a step towards her, hands in his pockets. 'Most governments try to keep it under wraps, but the archaeologists do find unsettling bits from time to time, things like the ledger and the graveyards. There are old texts, stories that would only make sense if we were mortal once.'

'You mean, if we all eventually contracted the Leak and simply died?'

'Exactly. With our antediluvian history lost, anyone can theorize, can't they? And this is why you and I are paid to stay holed up here: someone always digs something up and starts wondering—and eventually, they become enthralled with this idea of death as the true natural order. Some of them even find our little Institute and crawl to us, like Cybele did. For these people, the Leak is the ultimate confirmation of their theories.' He paused for the briefest second. 'I admire their perseverance, yet in the end I am a healer, just like you are. No matter what I think of their theories, I do not have the patience to entertain their madness.'

'What if they're right? What if this is the way we are meant to end? What if we were short-lived, once, so very long before the Floods that we had lost even the memory of it when the waters came?'

'Care to tell that to the people withering in the basement? That it is all right to suffer as they do, that they are doing their ancestors proud?'

No. The answer came unbidden and she silenced it, but it hung between them for a whole ripe moment before dissipating.

She held back for a second, then another. Finally, she sighed.

'What will happen to her?'

'It is never my decision. All I could do was tell the agents who came to question me that the Leak drives some of us mad and they should take pity on her, see her as another casualty of this disease. I doubt I made any difference, though. The last thing the government wants is more cultists.'

'Why hide this truth from us researchers, though? Why not tell us, a few decades in?' And then, 'Why not tell everyone in the world about this mortality theory? We are still a democracy, are we not?'

He was silent for a few seconds, and something of this silence crept into her bones.

'Because once the idea gets into someone's head that the Leak is the way things should be, Doctor, ugly things start to happen to the believers. The pull becomes stronger. More visceral. It tugs at people at a whole other level. And for those of us who have looked at a patient's eyes, the sensation becomes irresistible. Do you understand what I am saying?'

She could read between the lines well enough. 'We get sick

too.'

He gave no reply, yet she found the answer in his eyes, and it chilled her.

She did not want the Leak. She did not want to get sick and then waste away. How could she? How could anyone? How could anyone believe, that this horror was the natural order of things? Cybele had been mad to think so. This was a disease, and like every disease it had to have a cure.

'What should I do?'

'Work.' His smile startled her. It was not a pretty sight, like light coming down on old ruins. 'Work harder than before, to find the cure and prove your friend and the Pures, or any other cultist, wrong. Because if we don't find a cure, Doctor, if there isn't one, then they might be right and the moment you believe that will be a painful one.'

No, this could not happen. She had things to do, they all had. A bucket list. Fishing. She looked at him and then nodded, chrome fingers limp at her side.

'Good night, Doctor. I trust you will keep this entirely to yourself. Better not to place any more people in danger, don't you think so?'

'Of course.'

She escorted him out, and closed the door.

She would not tell, he was right about that. No reason to drag Milo and the rest into that. No reason to put them in such danger. She would sleep on it, then wake up and start working, really working. Now that she knew, she would request permission again to dig among the Institute's roots. This time, he would not have reason to deny her. She would find out why the Leak called to all of them, the real reason, not Cybele's delusions. After all, what else was left to do?

A chord a bit too deep, the Director had said. She went to pick the tablet, stare at the graves again, but stopped in her tracks.

Tomorrow would come and with it, questions. But tonight, the sky was clear and the Institute was silent. The world's buried truths could wait for one last, peaceful night.

Android Whores Can't Cry
Natalia Theodoridou

False start #1
MEETINGS AT MASSACRE MARKET
by Aliki Karyotakis
for the London New Times

I met Brigitte at what the locals call Massacre Market. She pronounced her name as if she were French—or I should say French-made, I guess, but I didn't know that at the time. She was a working girl, owned by a guy named Jerome—also French, supposedly. She was waiting there for my local liaison and me, among desiccated corpses and stalls full of blown-up photos of the tortured and the dead. She kissed Dick on the lips when she saw us, before greeting me. She did it in a mechanical way, as if she were supposed to, as if she couldn't do otherwise. That's when I saw the long strip of nacre that ran down the back of her neck, along her spine, pure and magnificent. I shot Dick a questioning look.

'Yeah yeah, it's the real deal,' he said. 'She's my artificial girlfriend in this town. I'm renting her full time. Very useful. She knows people.' Dick could be snide like that. 'I'm sure you girls will get along,' he added.

Brigitte turned to me, holding out her hand. She gave me a warm smile, but I could tell that she, unlike Dick, was very well aware of where we were, of the transactable images of gore and violence that surrounded us. Of the history of this place.

'Pleasure to meet you,' she said, a glint of something

indecipherable in her eye. Was that an android thing? Or was that the part of her that is human?

Androids can usually pass, if they don't have any visible nacre. But, of course, as soon as nacre appeared on android skin, people started wearing fake nacre patches as a fashion statement. When the patches are high quality you can't really tell them apart.

What was the nacre's appeal? I suppose part of it is that we still don't understand why or how it is formed. The other part is that it's perfect, beautiful. And that it doesn't perish.

Nacre is forever.

[Note to self: You sound like an infatuated schoolgirl. What does Brigitte have to do with anything? Get it together. Just get the facts straight. Also, preserve both Dick's and Brigitte's anonymity.]

END OF FILE

*

Nacre: Formation and Function

Nacre, or 'mother of pearl' is a composite material produced by certain molluscs as an inner shell lining and as the outer coating of pearls.[1] Since the APC-VII[2] finalized and started regulating the production of androids globally, nacre has been a standard feature of all artificially produced semi-mechanical humanoid organisms.[3] The production of android nacre had not been foreseen and remains unexplained. However, android nacre is considered harmless, if not beneficial for humans as an identifying mark, and so no attempts to avoid its appearance on android skin have been made.

Nacre formation is an evolutionary conserved and multiply-convergent process among the Mollusca phylum, arising as early as the Ordovician period (488 to 443 million years ago). While the exact process of its production is little understood even in nature, the function of natural nacre is largely defensive: layers of nacre protect the soft tissues of the organism from parasites, while damaging debris can be entombed in successive layers of nacre, ultimately resulting in the formation of a pearl.

The function of android nacre remains unknown.

#

[1]'Pearl' is also slang for a locally produced hallucinogenic that is sometimes used in meditation. Despite the name, the connection with either natural or android nacre has not been confirmed, largely due to lack of research.

[2]APC: Android Production Committee.

[3]These are commonly referred to as Androids, as this has been the popular term for many decades—however the universal applicability of the term has been questioned on various grounds. Still, other proposed terms, such as Gynoid and Cyborg, although more accurate in certain cases, are no longer in widespread use.

END OF FILE

*

Fieldnotes #1

It's Dick's afternoon playtime and he makes Brigitte re-enact scenes from his past while I try to work on my article. Playing in front of me is awkward, indiscrete. Vulgar, even. But I'm sure he does it on purpose—he *wants* me there. He wants me to witness this, and he knows I won't interfere. He is the client: his game, his rules.

Brigitte playacts Sandra, my college friend and Dick's ex-wife. She kinda looks like her too. Now they're acting out the night Sandra left him—left us. Dick is high on pearl. I can tell from that slightly unfocused look in his eyes. Like he sees things past Brigitte, past the windows and the smog, past the illusion of life.

'I can't be with you anymore,' Brigitte says. It sounds like she's said this line a hundred times already—a recitation. It seems she's in learning mode for these sessions. Dick is shaping her into Sandra. I find this deeply disturbing. 'You're such a brute,' Brigitte recites. 'Not sophisticated at all.'

'That's who I was when you married me. What was different then?'

Brigitte pretends to put all of her clothes in a suitcase, preparing to leave. Dick follows her around, practically yelling in her ear.

'I'll tell you what was different,' Dick says, 'you were a horny little cunt back then, weren't you.'

Brigitte stops packing and just stares at him.

'You're supposed to cry now,' Dick says, and then pretend-slaps his forehead. 'But I forgot. You can't cry, can you?' He turns to me. 'Hey Aliki, did you know that? Android whores can't cry. Because who wants to fuck a whiny bitch, right? Right?'

I look at Brigitte. I think I see a twitch disfigure her lips for the tiniest of moments, but then she smiles. 'Who wants to fuck a whiny bitch?' she repeats. Still in learning mode. Damn it.

'You really are a dick sometimes, Richard,' I say.

Dick laughs. He comes over and hugs me.

Brigitte keeps smiling, a twinkle in her eye.

END OF FILE

*

Nacre: Human Use

Historically, nacre has been prized for its iridescent appearance, while its strength and resilience has made it a suitable material for a variety of purposes. The nacreous shells of sea snails were used as gunpowder flasks in the 18th century and earlier. Nacre inlays have decorated some of the most renowned temples and palaces in Istanbul, traditional musical instruments in Greece, the keys of flutes, and the buttons of kings and queens the world over. Some accordion and concertina bodies are entirely inlaid with nacre. Little spoons made solely of nacre have been used to eat caviar in Russia, in order not to spoil the taste with metal.

All of these practices, although rarer, continue to this day. However, where natural nacre was used in the past, android nacre, the price of which is exorbitant due to the legal restrictions placed on its farming, is mostly used today.

[Note to self: I wonder what it feels like for androids. Do they consider nacre to be a part of their skin? A part of who they are? What would it feel like to see your skin as decoration, a musical instrument, a spoon?]

END OF FILE

*

False Start #2
MASSACRE MARKET: A HISTORY OF VIOLENCE AND
SILENCE
by Aliki Karyotakis
for the London New Times

'That great dust-heap called "history."'
Augustine Birrell

'Truth? I have no use for that. Truth won't feed my people. It
won't cover their bodies. Won't keep them safe.'
The General

My air-conditioned taxi drives me through the outskirts of the
city. I gaze in comfort at the unfinished highways, the hollow
skeletons of skyscrapers looming over them as a reminder of
the economic fallout—a city in perpetual suspension. But once
at the centre, this city is impeccable—polished and shiny, no sign
of poverty or suffering anywhere. It makes one think of the new
regime's necessity, its efficiency. A good alternative to the chaos
and agony that came before. Only the smog weighs on us, like a
bad omen.

As soon as I step out of the vehicle, I realize this is the hottest
and most humid part of the day; the smog is so thick I can hardly
breathe or make out any sky. My local liaison is meeting me in
front of the city pillar, the geographical and spiritual centre of
the city, from where everything extends outwards. I find out that
the Massacre Market is tucked away at the heart of a crowded,
semi-underground slum—the city's last. We have to get there on
foot. It will be a difficult journey.

When we arrive, hot and breathless, I am greeted by what my
liaison describes as 'The Political Cadaver of this country': the
dead body politic, the regime's atrocities mechanically reproduced
and exchanged in a gamble with the spirits of the dead, a funerary
protest. The place is crowded and dark and putrid; the stalls
exhibit small mountains of body parts and corpses—some fake,

some real (and I can't tell which is which)—the brownish hue of
decay accentuated by the bright orange robes of the monks and
nuns that frequent the place, looking for visual aids to their death
meditations. Tall cork-lined walls are covered by the forbidden
pictures of the massacred and those brutalized by police. Relatives
petrified in front of them, looking for the familiar face among
the myriads, looking but not wanting to find I'm sure, or making
small shrines with offerings for the disappeared; while protestors
and instigators pick out the most shocking ones to circulate and
share, to dub as the hidden reality of the regime, its true face
the face of those it murdered. In the loudspeakers, recordings
of the massacre's soundscape: screams and bullets, the sound of
revolting children and of a state devouring its young.

I spot a mother clinging to the image of her dead boy, his face
proliferated ad infinitum, plastering an entire wall, in protest.

Here, at Massacre Market, death is a political act.

[Note to self: People need the historical and political
background of the story to make sense of any of these. Start
with an interview instead? Also, explain Death Meditation.]

END OF FILE

*

The First Death Meditation

Death is certain.
      There is no way to escape death.
      We start dying the moment we are born.
      The body is a husk, a shell, an overcoat. It must be left behind.
      Imagine you are performing a vivisection on yourself.
      Imagine every detail.
      Concentrate on the repulsiveness of the human body.
      The corpse, swollen and bruised.
      The skin, peeled back.
      The fat, removed.
      The muscle, shredded.
      The organs, shrivelled and gone.
      The bones, pulverized.
      The corpse, festering. The corpse, fissured. The corpse,

gnawed. The corpse, dismembered, fragmented, scattered. The corpse, bleeding. The corpse, eaten by maggots and gone.

You remain.

END OF FILE

*

Interview with X, one of the leading protestors at the November Massacre

Part I [PLX1.vf]

Q: What is Massacre Market?

A: Images of death, disease and violence are forbidden by the regime; they are not good for foreign affairs, for the economy, won't bring in investments. So now there's a black market for that. It's not about money, though. We believe in an exchange of gifts with and for the dead. At the same time, it's a political thing. Because the government and the military want to hide the dead, when we photograph them and share their pictures, when we circulate footage of the massacres, we are exposing the true face of the regime. It's a form of protest.

Q: A protest against what?

A: Against the regime's suppression of the fundamental truths of life and death. Of poverty and suffering. Against the state's cover-ups of its core practices, the terrorizing and massacre of its own citizens when they dare to speak out or deviate in any way.

Q: Then how does Massacre Market survive? How come they haven't shut it down yet?

A: They have tried; they do raid it from time to time, but it pops up again after a while. Some people believe it is allowed to exist, or even that it has been set up by the government, as a safety valve, you know? To serve as an illusion of resistance.

Q: Do you believe that?

A: I do not.

Q: Can you talk about the November Massacre? I know this is the most recent one, but there have been others.

A: Yes, that is correct.

[He hesitates.]

Q: Can you recount the day of the Massacre?

A: [Pause] In the morning, the General was scheduled to appear at the city centre, very near the University. Attendance was, of course, mandatory, for students and first class citizens alike. So everyone gathered as planned. The General delivered the formal greeting and raised his arms in the usual salutation. The masses cheered, as expected, as they should. They couldn't do otherwise, you understand. But then, then, they kept on cheering. And clapping. Just cheering and clapping as loud as they could, whistling and cheering, and waving. And they wouldn't stop. After a few minutes, it became evident that this was no enthusiasm. It was super-conformity, you see? By cheering, they did not allow the General to speak. He literally couldn't get a word in. But what could he do? We were only applauding, he couldn't possibly punish us for that. So he mumbled the end of the speech he never managed to actually deliver, got off the podium and went back to wherever it is the General goes back to. And then the crowd was allowed to disperse, but the students and some others lingered. They were still not allowing themselves to talk, but they were smiling. They were shaking hands, not yet daring to speak about change, but that feeling, you know? That feeling, it was there. I felt it.

But then the trucks and the tanks appeared and sealed off the main square around the city pillar with the students still in it. We were surrounded before we realized what was going on. Some of us managed to slip through and save ourselves. Some holed themselves up inside the Polytechnic School at the University. They got them, though, eventually. They got them all.

Q: What did they do to them?

A: Why are you asking? You know very well what they did to them. You've seen the pictures, no? [Kneeling under the sun, hands tied, some behind their backs, some in front of their chests, beaten with steel batons and shiny black boots. Taken with a fisheye lens, they look like a human ocean. Innumerable, uncountable, and unaccounted for.] You've seen the footage. [Herded onto cattle-trucks by the back of their necks. Taken to that off-camera place from where no-one returns.] At four o'clock, it rained. The streets turned red.

[Pause] Of this, we will not speak.

[He takes a moment to find his bearings, he seems truly emotional. Then he adds:] They even destroyed several androids—most of them sex workers and cleaners—and later reimbursed their owners. I should say 'bribed,' to keep them from making a fuss.

Q: You said androids? Why were they there? Were androids part of the protest?

A: Yes, android guerillas have always been on our side, and uni students are often particularly drawn to them. There are several reasons for this. On the one hand, androids are part of the oppressed. They are low class, second rate, not even citizens. Most people don't even consider them persons. But there is also something about them that speaks of truth, not least their perfect, infallible memories. It's the human machine's trap: the freedoms afforded to them by what little flesh they possess and command, the failings of that same flesh... these are not so easy to tell apart. They do not decay, too, while our whole culture is premised on decay and death, or, now, on its concealment. Why do you think people are so crazy about those nacre patches? You've seen the ones?

[Note to Self: Transcribe the rest of the interview from voice file PLX2.vf]

END OF FILE

*

Fieldnotes #2

Getting people to talk is difficult. Brigitte and Dick work hard to find me the right contacts. But it takes time, and I know so little. I understand so little. This investigation is going to be long. We need to be discrete.

I often sit and watch Brigitte when she thinks I'm in my head, working, not paying attention to her.

She seems restless in her own skin, walking from the door to the window and back again. She stares outside at the smog—you can't see anything out the window, just grey and brown. Well, at least I can't. Maybe she can see something, maybe she can see everything. I don't know.

Her nacre has been multiplying the past few weeks. There is a new patch behind her left ear, and one on the back of her right hand—her most prominent still. It makes her look adorned.

When she catches me looking at her, the programming kicks in and she responds with her standard line, every time: 'What can I do for you, honey?' Then she lowers her eyes and looks embarrassed.

She's always lived here, and yet I can detect a faint French accent when she says this. Like some guy's fantasy of what a French whore should sound like.

END OF FILE

*

Some notes on the translation of Massacre Market

There is some uncertainty about the translation from the local language of what I have called 'Massacre Market.' Other possible translations include 'Atrocity Place,' 'Massacre Fair,' or, and that was the most confusing aspect of this, 'Pearl Fountain,' because even though each of the two words means something different, together they create a new compound which, as Dick and Brigitte explained to me, could rather clumsily be interpreted as 'a fountain whence pearls flow,' 'the breeding ground of oysters,' or even 'the plane of sublime imperfections.'

END OF FILE

*

Fieldnotes #3

Dick has started being rougher in his re-enactments; I doubt these are memories, no, I'm sure they are not, because these versions are conflicting and contradictory, and things happen that I know never really happened. Brigitte/Sandra is not always the one leaving him any more—sometimes he leaves her, sometimes she dies. Sometimes he kills her, chokes her. Or, he pretends to. He acts disinterested afterwards, says these are only stories he makes up and likes to play out; but I know, any reporter knows there are no disinterested stories, least of all the ones we tell ourselves.

Brigitte says she doesn't mind, she doesn't feel, remember? It's her job, she says. I'm still not convinced. I find myself in my reporter's role nonetheless, taking everything in, observing, reluctant to participate. This is not how the game is played, I tell myself.

I watch the nacre spread on her skin, covering more and more each day, like a disease of unbearable beauty.

'How did you end up in this mess, anyway?' Dick asked me yesterday. 'I never thought they'd send a woman.'

I hit him hard on the arm and he laughed. 'I choose not to be insulted,' I said. 'Anyway, I needed this. Badly. Went through a rough patch a while back and was out of circulation for some time. So when I went back to my boss and begged, he gave me the case nobody else would take.'

Dick stopped fiddling with his cigarettes and turned to me. I had his full attention now, and I wasn't sure I wanted it. I shouldn't have said anything.

'Rough? How rough?' he asked.

I said nothing.

'You know you can talk to me, right?'

I thought of his hands around Brigitte's neck. *What happened to you, Richard? You were a tender boy, back then.*

'It's been a while, Dick. I'm sorry.'

I think I hurt his feelings, but he tried not to show it. And at that moment I realized I didn't mind. Hurting him. I didn't mind at all.

END OF FILE

*

The Second Death Meditation

The second meditation rehearses the actual death process.

Engage now in this series of yogas, modelled on death.

First, the body becomes very thin, the limbs barely held together. You will feel that the body is sinking into the earth. Your sight becomes blurry and obscured. You may see mirages. Do not believe them. The body loses its lustre.

Then, all the fluids in the body dry up. Saliva, sweat, urine, blood dry up. Feelings of pleasure and pain dry with them. You may feel like smoke.

Then, you can no longer hear. You cannot digest food or drink. You do not remember your name, or the names of the ones you knew and loved. You cannot smell. You may not be able to inhale, but you will be able to exhale.

Then, the ten winds of the body move to your heart. You will no longer inhale or exhale. You will not be able to taste. You will not care. The root of your tongue will turn blue. You may feel like a lamp about to go out.

Then, nothing.

Then, nothing.

Then, nothing. The ten winds dissolve. The indestructible drop at the heart is all that remains.

END OF FILE

*

Fieldnotes #4

'Why do you let him treat you like that?' I ask her almost reflexively one day. I regret it right away. Am I blaming her for the way he treats her? Shouldn't I be blaming him?

She thinks about it for a while, then shrugs.

'It's my job,' she says. 'I don't have a choice. Some things are in my programming.'

'Yes, but some aren't.'

She looks me in the eyes, fixes her gaze there, and she seems less human than ever before. People don't look at others like that. 'I'm a whore,' she states.

'You are more than a whore. It's not who you are. It's simply what you do.'

'See, you got it backwards. What we are for is who we are. A hammer is what a hammer does. Would you ever use a hammer to screw a screw or cut a piece of wood?'

'Just a tool, then.'

'That's right. Just a tool.'

'Doesn't my saying that offend you?'

'Do you think it should?'

I don't say anything.

'Why?' she continues. 'We are all tools for something. Aren't you? It's not an android thing. It's an existential thing.'

I lower my eyes.

She leans over and touches my shoulder. 'I'm sorry,' she says. 'Sometimes empathy is difficult for me. We don't feel anything, you know. No feelings.'

She seems sincere, but I don't believe her; I tell her so. 'Some people say the nacre is a byproduct of the things you do feel that were not programmed. Just like the nacre wasn't, and yet, there it is.'

She shrugs again. 'My programming allows me to imitate feeling and to learn from other people's perceptions of me. No one knows what the nacre is, or what it does.' She pauses for a bit. Then she adds: 'Perhaps it's a form of rust. Tools do rust, don't they?'

END OF FILE

*

My trip

I'm sitting by the window, looking out. The smog seems heavier today. Darker, too. I think it's the colour of rot. I wish I could see past it. I wish I could see.

Brigitte comes home—I notice there is a bright new patch of nacre under her right eye. She smiles, like she always does.

'Get dressed,' she says. 'I need to show you something.'

When I'm ready to go, she holds out her hand closed in a fist. Slowly, she uncurls her fingers and reveals a pearl resting on her palm. It takes me a couple of seconds to realize what it is, and then I look at her, trying to figure out what she's planning.

'Put this under your tongue, Aliki,' she says. 'You'll see. You'll understand.'

I put the pearl in my mouth and we set out into the smog and that corpse of a city.

We are at the main square. The pearl is still dissolving under my tongue; it tastes sweet and tangy and makes my heart beat irregularly. I see the city pillar towering over us—round and bulging at the bottom, thinning as it reaches for the sky. The top disappears into the thick layers of smog above. Its marble surface emits a subdued light, like a fading beacon.

'It was built hundreds of years ago as a mystical axis around which the city would be born, you know,' Brigitte says. 'The story of its construction is now largely ignored and forgotten, but spirit mediums still gather here sometimes. They consider it a source of power for those who commune with the dead. It is said that when the foundation for the pillar was laid, a fosse was dug around it. They brought every young pregnant slave girl they could find, slit their throats and threw them in there to die, and through their death empower the pillar to protect the city.'

I look at the base of the pillar and realize I am standing on top of where the trench would have been, if that story were true. The pillar starts glowing brighter and brighter and I look up to see if the sun has somehow penetrated the smog. I feel the ground shake under my feet, then give, and I fall into the trench. The slave girls are there, all around me, with their blood still seeping into the earth, their fetuses still dying in their wombs.

This city is built on gore. The shiny marble, a tombstone laid over history. I see the streets turn into veins. I see students parade through the city with what corpses they could salvage; they carry them on their shoulders, their friends, their classmates, their lovers, displaying them like a mute witness to the regime's moral order. And then these students are shot down or snatched off the streets, the corpses torn from their arms. They are strung on trees and shot, or burnt alive, or worse. Of this, we will not speak.

The body is nothing. Its image, everything.

Brigitte pulls me away. She leads me through the city's red streets, the ten winds of its body dying down. I think Brigitte is speaking to me. I think she says:

'Let's look for the indestructible drop at the heart.'

We are descending. She is walking in front of me, showing me the way. The nacre on her skin seems brighter than ever. I dare touch it for the first time—I reach out and brush my fingers against the back of her neck, tracing the nacre down her spine. I didn't expect it to be so hard. 'You are indestructible,' I mutter, or I think I do, and she turns around and smiles.

We are at Massacre Market. It has changed since the first time I saw it; it seems even more crowded now, the walls of photographs fuller, covered once, and then covered again by more pictures, and more on top of those, layer upon gory layer, corpse upon corpse, body part upon body part. The desiccated corpses seem more real now, almost alive, absurd. Brigitte tells me something I don't hear; her voice drowns in the screams and static spilling from the loudspeakers.

One of the photographs on the wall next to me catches my eye. I walk closer—it's grainy, black and white, but I can still see the girl: she is laid out in a field next to others, dozens of others. Her top is removed, her chest slashed open. 'Foreign slut' is written on her bare belly. She looks like a younger version of myself. *This is me*, I think, *this is me, years ago. Why don't I remember this?* I put my palm on the photograph—what did I want to do? Cover her up, I suppose—and I notice a patch of nacre spreading between my fingers. I pull my hand back as if the photo suddenly burnt me and I watch the nacre spread. I feel it cover my entire body, and I'm calcified, my skin adorned and indestructible. 'I feel like an instrument,' I shout to Brigitte over the sound of massacre, 'like an accordion, or a concertina.' *Play me like a flute, O Lord*, I think.

Brigitte tries to tell me something, but I can't make it out. I struggle to read her lips. '...it disappoints...' I hear, but the rest is stifled by static, and she's far away. I see her pointing at my arms from afar. I look down and see the nacre growing dull and flaking, then my skin peeling and falling off, the fat exposed, the muscle, the bone, and I know, I know then, this city is a skin, no blood anywhere in sight, all surface, all shine and the slightest glimpse of nacre here and there—is it real? Is it not? Does it make a difference?

END OF FILE

*

False Endings

I have precious little time left. So I will not say much. One never has the skin that befits her.

I know I'll never finish this article—I still haven't even decided on the title, or what this story is really about. What do you think? I might have called it:

Massacre Market

or

The Mechanical Reproduction of Violence: Truth, Massacre, History

or even

Android Whores Can't Cry: Under the Surface of Death Meditation

Either way, I know that, if I did finish it, I would dedicate it 'To my B., my pearl, who taught me this:

The skin always disappoints.'

END OF FILE

*

END OF RECORD. 14 OF 14 FILES RECOVERED.

*

This is all the material I managed to retrieve from Aliki's hard drives. I wait for the reporter sitting across from me in Dick's living room to go through them.

'You realize your memory files provide conflicting information about what happened to both my colleague Aliki Karyotakis and her informant Richard Phillips,' he says.

I am silent. Is that true?

I recall the last time I saw Aliki.

She is lurching at Dick, pushing him away from me during one of his violent playacts. He falls back and hits his head. He is very still. We are all very still.

She is also standing by the city pillar with me, in a crowd of people I haven't quite registered. I look at the sky. The sun is shining through the smog. When I look down again, she's gone.

She is also looking at me as a tall man leads her onto a platform and places a hood over her head. Then a noose. Then the platform gives.

She was also never here. I never met her.

And Dick? Dick is always either dead or missing.

'Have you tinkered with your memory?' *the reporter asks.*

'It is possible,' *I say.* 'But I have no memory of that, as I am sure you are aware.'

'Of course.' *He shuffles in his chair.* 'OK, let's take the first version. Can you tell me what happened?'

He already knows this. Why does he ask?

'She pushed him. He died. Humans break easily like that.'

'And then?'

'She turned herself in.'

'Wasn't she terminated?' *That's when I notice the nacre on his underarm. Ah.*

'I think the human term is 'sentenced to death and executed',' *I correct him. He should know this. I'm sure he does.*

'Did you watch? The execution, I mean.'

I watch him. He is serious, eyes cold. A reporter reports.

'A hammer is what a hammer does,' *I whisper.*

'Excuse me?'

'Nothing,' *I say.* 'A reflex. Yes. Yes, I think I watched.' *I sense the nacre spread on my face, my surface irreparably hardened. It reflects the light so brightly it almost hurts my eyes.*

'Are you going to cry?' *he asks, hoping, I bet, for a good twist in his story.*

The programming takes over, like gears shifting inside me, and I can't stop it I can't stop it I can't.

'Android whores can't cry,' *I say.* 'Who wants to fuck a whiny bitch?'

This puzzles him. He focuses on my lips, and he's about to say something, but he stops. I know he stops because of what he sees. He looks disappointed.

I feel the nacre cover my lips and I realize this was the last time I spoke. This shouldn't be happening so fast. I think of freedoms and failings. I am not sure which is which. It doesn't matter. I am the oyster and the pearl. I am a shell that doesn't speak.

I wonder what really happened to her, what happened to Dick. I know I'll never know—and this somehow strikes me as appropriate. The truth has seeped through the pores on the skin of the city. Aliki is in its bloodstream now. So is Dick. So is the core of this story.

I remain.

The Colour that Defines Me
Stamatis Stamatopoulos

Translator from Greek language: Stephanie Polakis

The Artist

When she came into the shop, I was slinging ink on a customer's tongue. The tat depicted a light blue sun; to me, of course, it looked light grey. She wanted her mouth to shine in her own personal colour, even when it was closed. Can you picture that?

Not that I'm judgmental of my customers' choices. I'll do whatever looney design they desire.

When the colours were lost after '48, no one imagined that tattooing would become one of the most lucrative jobs. Even the past seven years of war hadn't managed to dent the trade. No one yearned to view a monotonous grey in the mirror; and having found your personal hue, a distinctive design and a bit of inox sparkling here and there made you happy to see your face, your body, your tongue.

Anyway.

I watched her as she was glancing at the designs on the wall. She was hot, at least twenty years younger than me, around twenty five. Born in the 50s, she belonged to the generation that had never seen colours. Light grey hair – the dirty blond of another era – about the same height as me, five nine, fit.

'Have a seat. I'll be with you in a moment.' I pushed out a little more ink and turned off the gun.

'Thinithed?' the customer asked. The xylocaine would take a

while to wear off.

'Yes.' I helped her to her feet.

She stuck her tongue out in the mirror and then smiled. 'I thucking wock!' she shouted.

I smiled back. It was nice to see someone appreciating your art. She paid and then it was just me and the stranger in the shop. As I approached her I could see that she had fixed up her body, as well. Flames the colour of graphite shot out from under her halter top, burning her back, chest and shoulders and licking at her neck. Her face was clean, without any tattoos or piercings.

'Impressive tattoo,' I said. 'Is that your colour?'

She looked at her reflection in the mirror. 'Yes,' she answered, with a bitter smile.

'I'm Kleanthes.' I extended my hand.

'Azure' she said, reaching out. A discreet perfume enveloped me, which awoke long forgotten images of colourful flowery meadows. Her grip was firm.

'Nice name. What can I do for you?'

'I'm looking for a tattoo.' She had a clear, deep voice, with a touch of sorrowful dark blue in it.

'You've come to the right place.'

'I hope so. It's the eighth shop I've been to.' She reached into a thin leather bag slung over her shoulder, pulled out a design and handed it to me.

I examined the motif, which was very simple, not at all inspired. Seven vertical stripes in different shades of grey, each about one centimetre wide, equally spaced, with various combinations of letters, symbols and numbers written on them. Stretched vertically under the stripes were three barbed wires.

I tried not to frown. 'This is for you? What you've got is far superior to this one. Why would you want to change it?'

'It's not for me.'

'To be honest this isn't even fit for a gift, either.'

'It isn't a gift. I'm looking for someone who has this on his right arm.'

That changed things. Only cops asked for things like that. Pulling away I lost the smile and gave back the design.

She smiled. 'I'm not a cop.'

'Even so, I can't help you.'

'Can't or won't?'

'How do I know if the person you're looking for wants to be found?'

She looked me in the eyes. 'The colour I see, the colour of the flames that burn my skin. I saw it for the first time in his eyes.'

I couldn't possibly know if this was true, but I certainly hadn't heard a more beautiful reason for wanting to find someone.

I must have had a distrustful look on my face. She said, 'Please.'

'And how come you didn't get to know him then?'

'I was fifteen years old. I was shocked. It was the first time I ever saw colour.'

I sighed and examined the design once more. I wondered who would get such a tattoo. No inspiration, definitely not made by any tattoo artist I knew, but I had seen it somewhere before. 'I hope you're telling me the truth.'

I disappeared into the workshop and returned with four dossiers filled with tattered transparent folders. 'I keep a record of all the designs I see' I said. I handed one to her and we started to flip through the folders. Most of them have hand drawn designs. Only a few are photos. Times are still hard and printing is expensive.

'I found it,' she cried after a few minutes, and turned the dossier so that it faced me.

A design much like hers was inside a clear folder. Instead of barbed wire five snakes slithered beneath the stripes.

I removed the design from its folder and turned it over. On the back, it read: 'Paint it Black Bar, November 2078'. Eight months ago. I showed it to Azure.

'Is that where you saw it?' she asked and gave it back to me.

'I haven't been there for ages. A customer of mine took me there a couple of months after the war ended. Had just opened. They served beer, and spirits they distilled themselves. I saw the tattoo on a guy. It wasn't anything special, but the stripes got my attention. They were perfectly parallel and the shading was very clear and distinctive. Even I have trouble doing that.'

'Was he older than me? Around thirty?'

I nodded. 'You know,' I looked at the design again, 'he had the same tattoo on his face too. Maybe he's not who you're looking for.'

For a moment, I thought I saw a puzzled look in her eye.

'That's him,' she said. 'What else can you tell me?'

I took a moment to think. 'It's possible that one of the stripes was his colour.'

'Did he look at it a lot?' she asked.

'Yes, he kept turning his wrist to look at his forearm.'

She nodded. 'Where is the bar?'

'Downtown, behind the American embassy.' I handed her the design she'd shown me.

'Thank you very much, Kleanthes. I'd started to think that I'd never find him.'

'I hope you do, and I hope it's everything you expect it to be.'

'Of that, I'm sure.' The way she said this made me think that she would have gladly tagged on an 'unfortunately.'

'Just because the first time you saw your colour was in his eyes, doesn't mean you owe him anything.'

She shifted her gaze downwards then immediately looked up again into my eyes. 'On the contrary, I owe him everything.' She turned to leave.

'Azure,' I called as she stepped out the door, 'what is your colour? What's the colour of his eyes?'

She glanced at her reflection in the glass door. 'They told me it is like the colour of honey.'

'That's a beautiful colour and a colour belongs to none.'

'I know,' she said gloomily. 'I know.'

She shut the door, and I never saw her again.

*

Ever since Maria died, Mohammad Asiyar wakes up very early, usually around four in the morning. And since he has neither a hobby nor any interests to keep him busy and alert, his mornings are spent torturously on his veranda.

During those few hours till sunrise, he sips his tea watching the sky turn from solid black to charcoal and finally ash grey, thinking about how he misses her white hair. He misses other things as well - her voice, her judgmental look when he forgot himself and ate with his mouth open, her hand in his when they took Sunday walks in the Ancient Agora. Nevertheless, it is her snowy hair he misses the most.

Since the colours were lost in '48, he never searched for his own, or stumbled upon it by chance. Maria's white hair had always been all the colours of the world to him.

White is not a special colour. Everyone could discern it, like everyone could see black. Mohammad is sharing his colour with everyone else, but he never cared, as long as Maria was there. But now, she's gone, and he's afraid. Her white is not there to soothe him, to defy the dullness of a colourless world. His memory fades, carrying away her brightness and his interest in living.

He's afraid of what will happen when he will no longer be able to bring that unique white in front of him. He's afraid because he doesn't know if finding a personal shade will revive him or if it will ruthlessly pollute his eyes with shredded memories of a world long gone.

That morning, when the car stops in front of the building's entrance below, he bends over the railing and looks, as he does at anything that happens in those empty hours of the day. And he is stunned when a young man gets out of the car and rings his door bell.

As he enters the flat to answer, he feels his heart pounding. 'Yes?' says through the intercom.

'Mr. Mohammad Asiyar?'

'Yes.'

'My name is Kita Markakis, and I was sent by Violet Dima. I'm her colleague. She would like you to come with me.'

Violet. He hasn't heard from her since Maria's funeral, and for her to send someone round at this hour can only mean one thing.

'Give me five minutes, and I'll be down,' says Mohammad, and rushes to get ready.

The Merchant

She found me through Argyris, one of my colleagues. Well, let's say he's a colleague; from time to time he pushes some of my stuff. He told me she was his cousin. I wouldn't have cared even if she was his mother. She wanted something I had to offer and I never say no to business, no matter how insignificant it is. Competition is too tough.

Baou, my bodyguard, showed her to my office. The asshole was slobbering all over her. Like he couldn't get it from the club's dancers any time he wanted. Even so, you always want what you can't have. And she was well worth it. A nice piece; classy. She had an air of sophistication, with a touch of severity. There was a tattoo on her body that perfectly suited her attitude, as if it were saying, 'Keep your distance or I'll burn you.' Easy to imagine her as the main attraction of the club.

'Mr. Lahoi, this is Azure Halkea, Argyris's cousin,' Baou said and took his place beside the office door.

Azure. Her parents must have been the kind of people who became melancholic after '48. Those people who named their kids after colours, like that would make any difference. Lost causes that would commit suicide by the dozens.

She came in and sassily approached the desk. She was wearing a mini dress with a wide belt and a carmen neckline that revealed her shoulders, all of which were the colour of ash. She carried a thin leather bag, one of those in which women manage to fit their entire existence.

'Have a seat,' I said.

'Do you have what I requested?' she asked, and she crossed her legs.

I opened up the humidor and offered her a cigar. She declined. I took one, cut the end and lit it. 'The tattoo is a military technique. It's given to members of Special Forces units. Every unit is made up of seven to eight people. Every stripe has a special colour that corresponds to each member's shade. It's a kind of identification, so that they don't kill each other. The numbers and letters are shade and unit codes.'

I took a puff of my cigar and blew out the smoke. 'Any other tattoos, they've engraved by themselves, allegedly without anaesthetic. Military macho bullshit, if you ask me.'

She didn't seem bothered by my language. 'What about the other matter?' she asked.

I opened the cupboard by the desk and took out a small long metal box that was the shade of coal. I put it down in the middle of the desk.

She went to pull the box towards her, but I put my hand over it. 'The information's free.'

She opened her bag and took out a wad of bills, which she then dropped on the desk.

I took it and started counting.

She opened the box and pulled out the contents: a metal cylinder, the same shade as its container, with a few numbers engraved on it and a trigger button on the top.

I finished counting. It was all there. 'That's it.' I said to her. 'You pull the bottom part until you hear a click. Then you turn it until the small arrow reaches the time you want and then you push the bottom part to lock it in place.'

'Like this?' she asked me.

'Yes. Now, all you have to do is press the trigger on the top. The amount of time you set is how long it takes to explode.'

She stared at me.

'Once you've pressed it,' I said to her calmly, 'there's no turning back.'

For a few moments we remained silent. I wondered what she was waiting for. She was lucky I was in a good mood, otherwise I might have taken the grenade and beaten the shit out of her.

I took another puff. The pleasure is double when you've got the upper hand. 'Of course, without this, you won't get the desired effect,' I said and revealed a small metal vial that I had in my jacket pocket.

I glanced at the grenade and gestured towards the box.

She chose to put the grenade in her bag.

I gave her the vial. 'I never give my clients an armed weapon. Especially those who seem to have a grudge against the entire world.' I smiled. 'The shaft is turned and comes off. After that...'

'I know.' She placed the vial in her bag, as well. 'Thank you, Mr Lahoi.' She stood.

'Always at your service.' I followed her. Baou opened the door for us. 'I never ask my clients what they do with what I provide them, but you aren't like the others.'

'You'd do well not to ask.'

'Special forces and formic chemical fragments. A dangerous combination. I wish I could believe you know what you're doing.'

'Mr. Lahoi, have you found your colour?'

I turned unwittingly and looked at the small ragged doll that I had on my desk. It shone pink against the grey. 'Yes.'

'So have I,' she responded, smiling. Her dark eyes were shining.

'What does that have to do with anything?'

She didn't answer. She just turned and left.

Baou took a step to follow her.

'Make sure she doesn't arm the grenade in the club,' I told him.

He nodded.

Craziness was certainly alive and kicking during the age of colours, but now it doesn't even bother to disguise itself. Which isn't bad for business.

The night fades away as the car heads for the General Hospital. Mohammad and Kita aren't talking much. There isn't much to say between an old retired cop and a new recruit.

Reflected in the windows of the car, images of the wounded city are changing rapidly before them. Mohammad shifts uncomfortably. This place is as old and hurt as he is. War has left its mark. He tries to remember, to evoke the old view. His mind is suddenly awakened, as rusted memories emerge.

It is March of 2070. Mohammad is in his office at the police headquarters.

A few yards away, a colonel is looking through the glass door at the teenage girl sitting outside the office. The weather is still cold and he is wearing a long trench-coat with shiny stars and small medals pinned onto it. 'Do you think that in a short time three deaths will matter?' the colonel asks, but not because he expects a reply. 'Nobody will remember them. The war has already begun. Everybody knows this, although most people still don't want us to participate.' He is making an effort to sound solemn. 'I understand them. I agree with them. I hope something will change at the last minute. I hope it will pass us by without knocking on our front door. But we must be prepared.'

The man's voice sounds steady and sure, making Mohammad think in disgust that the colonel is trained to inspire people to do the unthinkable; because war is on their doorstep - the 'War of Colours' - how ironic. The colours were lost twenty-two years before the conflict even started. In this war, the blood that will be shed won't be red, but black.

The detective feels more tired with every word. I should send him to hell, he thinks. He gets up out of his desk chair and approaches the colonel. Guarding the girl is Violet, newly recruited on the force. But if he's right?

'I promise you, if that bastard comes back alive, I will turn him in myself so that he can pay for his sins,' the colonel continues his monologue. He turns to Mohammad. 'For the time being though, do me a favour and freeze the case. He's on a mission, anyway.'

The war hasn't officially started and a maniac has already taken his first victims. In this war, he most certainly will be useful.

'Are we in agreement, detective?'

Mohammad feels an urge to say something. He is in his office, not in the colonel's. There has to be a response that will fix everything. But his mind is stuck on one thought, if he's right...

The colonel opens the door and leaves.

The young woman observes him as he walks down the corridor, then looks at Mohammad. Her wet gaze traps him. Somehow she already knows, but unfortunately, this doesn't mean he will escape from having to give her the awful news.

'Azure, come in sweetie,' says Mohammad. He feels tired and he'd prefer being somewhere else, but he has no choice.

He is here and he has to end this.

Kita kills the engine and steps out of the car. They've reached the hospital.

The Barwoman

The everyday greyness might have been something inevitable, like the rising and the setting of the sun, were it not for a damn random and personal colour that we all found at some point to remind us of what we had lost decades ago. To remind us that some of us had been born after the fact.

For this reason, my job at 'Paint it Black' is neither a mundane nor a tiring activity. I work in a place full of music, where people come to get away from their troubles. Even if they don't want to, some alcohol and a few happy faces help most of them to leave their problems at the door. Those who aren't capable of letting go usually don't return. They can't stand it.

That night, the place was crowded, but not packed, and I wouldn't have noticed her, except she sat on my side of the bar. She set her bag down and I leaned over to take her order. From the speakers, a guy was sorrowfully singing: 'They give you this, but you pay for that.'

'Pour me your colour.'

I was quite taken aback. How could she possibly know my colour?

She smiled at me and raised her shoulders, like she was answering my question.

'OK,' I replied and grabbed the green vodka. 'How did you know?' I inquired as I filled a glass in front of her.

'Intuition,' she answered.

'Come on...'

'It's true.' She gave me a wink and took a sip. 'Azure,' she said and extended her hand.

'Flora.' I accepted the handshake. 'Now you're going to tell me that you know what colour I see...'

'Green,' she answered and my jaw fell. 'You're lucky. Your parents really nailed the colour.'

I laughed. 'That's crazy! How did you know that?'

'It says so on the label.'

'Alright. That was easy. Tell me though, how did you know that a drink has my colour?'

'I've been here a couple other nights and it's the only thing you drink. Always straight up and you always look at it in a strange way. A combination of love and hate, I'd say.'

That was it. I liked her.

The night went on. I served the customers, but I always returned to Azure. 'Nice tattoo,' I remarked at some point.

'It sort of looks like yours.'

Indeed it did. Both covered the same areas, but mine had thorny stems with flower buds on the ends.

'To beautiful pictures that hurt us,' she said, raising her glass.

I agreed and took a sip of mine.

At around twelve o'clock, Carmine, the boss, arrived. He motioned to me from the other side of the bar and I went to see what he wanted, leaving Azure alone for a bit. When I got back, she stared at him as he was walking to his office on the first floor. 'Are you OK?'

After a moment, she turned to me. 'Yes.'

'Are you sure?'

'Can you pour me another?' She pushed her glass in my direction.

Her attitude had changed completely and I couldn't understand why. Up until that moment, we were having a great time and I was afraid that I'd done something to offend her. I'd find out later that evening just what had caused this reaction.

For the next half hour, I couldn't get one word out of her. Then suddenly she asked me how long I've been working here.

'About six months,' I answered.

'The décor is cool.'

I looked around me. The walls were covered in graffiti with the titles of songs from the previous century. Perhaps it had helped that the EMP bombs had destroyed all the contemporary storage devices, leaving only old CDs and DVDs untouched.

Brown Sugar, Red Red Wine, Back in Black, Yellow Submarine, Grey Day, Crimson and Clover, White Rabbit. The colours were written in giant fonts. I liked that background, too.

'You should have seen it a few months ago. It was a real shithole. The boss did a really good job.' I was kind of relieved she was talking to me again.

'Did he design it?'

I rolled my eyes. 'He's not capable. He just placed his trust in the right people.'

'He sounds like a smart person. Has he been in the business a long time?'

'I don't think so. From what I've heard, he was probably in the army.'

'Really?' she asked. 'At least he's doing something with his life now.'

It is common knowledge that most veterans who survived the war returned to an unfriendly world.

'He's doing his best,' I replied.

'Was he the guy you spoke to before?'

'Yes, that was him.'

'You know, Flora,' she said, 'I don't have a job at the moment. Do you need some extra help? Do you think I could talk to him?'

I thought about it for a second. The club was doing real well and business was getting better and better every month. It was just a matter of time until Carmine would hire another person. Why not Azure?

'Normally, I wouldn't do this for someone I met a couple of hours ago.'

'Thanks, Flora. You're a lifesaver.'

'It's no big deal.' At that moment, I didn't think I was doing anything important.

I told her to wait, asked a colleague to cover for me, then went upstairs. I spoke to Carmine and came back down to the bar. 'Go upstairs. He's expecting you.'

She squeezed my hand and smiled. She looked straight into my eyes, grabbed her bag and turned to go.

'You can do it,' I called after her.

'I know,' she replied. She wasn't smiling this time.

I watched her as she moved away. Every few steps, she would pause and glance at someone or something. A young girl dancing, a couple kissing, someone laughing. A bit later, she disappeared into the back rooms of the club. When I saw her again, she had completely changed.

*

A couple of police cars and ambulances are parked in the hospital yard. Nearby, hospital staff are smoking and drinking their coffee. They glance at Mohammad as he gets out of the car.

Kita points to a building. 'Second floor.'

The old man stares towards the entrance. He knows exactly what awaits him inside. Closure is desirable but not always inviting.

A few minutes later, he arrives at the second-floor reception desk, where

Violet is waiting for him.

'Good morning, Mohammad,' she greets him with a smile. It isn't the same warm smile she used to offer him when they worked together. She'd rather he was anywhere but here.

Mohammad sympathizes with her.

'Please forgive me for bringing you out at such a time, but...'

'I know,' he cuts her off.

The smile disappears. She looks him in the eye.

'The Halkea Case?' he asks.

She nods. 'We are in the dark. We need the missing links.'

'I want full access afterwards.'

'I can't...'

'You know better than anyone, Violet. Isn't that why you brought me here?'

She doesn't answer. She just smiles; in a familiar way.

'Can I go in now?'

'Room 212.'

He turns and heads down the corridor. A policeman is sitting outside the room. Violet gestures to him from a distance and the guard lets him pass.

Mohammad slowly opens the door. The only light in the room comes from a small nightlight on the wall, the rest of the room is shrouded in darkness.

He enters and closes the door behind him.

The Soldier

That day marked the one-month anniversary of the last time I saw my colour. A month is neither a long time nor a short time. And I'd be relishing its absence. *Don't be disillusioned.* But this time, the absence had begun after one more misstep. So a month meant nothing whatsoever.

When Flora left, I sat at my desk and opened the drawer. I looked at its contents and started to justify what I wanted to do. White sheets of paper, a stapler, a small dagger, a roll of tape, a tube of glue, pencils, pens, white-out, ink, wax and matches. *Just a thin line, Carmine.* Deep inside, I knew that every one of my rationalizations was a load of crap. Despite my efforts to distance myself from anything that enticed me, there was always some deeper self, someone who was well-trained at lurking, who managed to camouflage temptations and place them right in front of me.

A whole month. That's a long time, Carmine. See a bit of colour. Just enough to get us straight, so we can get through another month. A thousand excuses to get off track one more time and only one plea to hold out: Don't do it. How feeble it seemed.

Luckily for Azure, she knocked on the door just seconds before I surrendered to temptation. Time had slipped by. If she had come a few minutes later, things may have turned out differently.

'Come in,' I said and slammed the drawer shut. When she entered, I had a smile across my face. Suddenly, I found the entire scene amusing. *Lady luck is on our side.*

She closed the door behind her. I didn't recognize her immediately. I saw a very pretty woman with a flame-covered cleavage. *What would our colour look like on her?*

'You must be Azure,' I said. 'Please, have a seat.'

For a moment, she looked upset. I thought she might open the door and leave. Nevertheless, she took a step, and then another step, and sat in the chair in front of the desk.

I was still smiling. She, though, was somewhat sombre. At first, I mistook her expression for hesitation and modesty. *We're scaring her.* But she was looking straight into my eyes with such intensity that memories started to flood my mind.

'You don't remember me,' she stated flatly. And then she added, 'I find it very sweet and precious.'

At her words a memory hit me so hard that it slammed me into the back of my chair. 'Impossible,' I managed to mumble.

'Is Carmine your real name?'

'It is,' I said. *What does she want? Our eyes!* In my head, my thoughts were racing. *You shouldn't have let her go.* 'You've grown.' What a stupid thing to say, but in my mind, she had remained a teenager.

'I survived.' There wasn't a shred of fear in her voice.

'How did you find me?'

'It wasn't easy. The war erased your tracks. But every monster like you gets messy eventually.'

Her last words brought me to my senses. She was the only one who had escaped my colour. *Don't waste any more time.*

She put her hands in her bag. *What are you waiting for?* My adrenaline piled up but I didn't stop her. I didn't want to, at least not yet. This encounter was like no other.

She produced a folder and threw it on the desk. I opened it. Inside, there were newspaper cuttings. I took one out. It was an article dated February referring to the murder of a young prostitute. Nora. Just one more woman who fell victim to post-war poverty. I pulled out another cutting. A homeless man was found butchered near the highway, just outside the city. *Alcohol and layers of filth.* One by one, I took out the rest of the cuttings: four more deaths. They were similar in nature. The victims were immigrants, beggars, drug addicts and were murdered around the city right after the war. *They wouldn't be missed.*

'How were you sure?' I asked. *You made mistakes, Carmine.*

'I discovered what your colour is.'

'And now what?' *She came to kill us.*

She didn't reply.

'If it has even the slightest significance, I want you to know that I'm sorry.' *No. You're not.* 'If I could change what I am, if I could bring back your parents and your sister, I would.' *And then you would do exactly what you did anyway.* 'But I am what I am. I see what I see.' *You like what we like.*

'I couldn't care less.' The intensity in her voice was growing. Her eyes were shining, tearing up.

'Then why did you come?'

'I want to hear you say how important your colour is to you. I want you to tell me that it defines who you are, your entire life. That without it, you're nothing.' She could barely contain her rage. Tears were streaming down her cheeks.

I took a deep breath: 'I confess that in my youth there were times when the sight of blood made me feel like the king of the world. Not any more. But that doesn't mean that it has ceased to be the most beautiful thing around me. It's a gift and a curse, but it's what I've got and I wouldn't ever change it.' *Half-truths,*

Carmine. Just before she came, I was ready to cut myself again for a line of warm blood. One month ago I'd killed again and I'd felt the same pleasure as always. However, I knew that with every life I took, I removed colours from this dreary world. *Oh, how I miss the alibi of war.*

'Once, they told me that I see a shade of red,' I said calmly. 'Red, crimson, scarlet; words from a different time.' *Lost words; misplaced, insignificant words.* 'For me, this is the colour that gushes forth. The only colour that exists is blood.' *Blood.* 'That night, you told me that in my eyes you saw something sweet and precious. I still don't know what colour my eyes are and no matter what name they told you to call it, I'm sure that there is none more suitable than the one you told me before I spared your life.'

'Sweet and precious,' she said as she started sobbing, 'is what *you* wanted to hear. The colour I first saw in your face, a face painted pitch-black with the blood of my family, was despicable and beastly; whenever I see that colour, I hurt. It's a curse. A curse that I have borne for years, something that reminds me of what you did to us.'

Tears ran down her face and her voice was hoarse. It was truly a sad spectacle. *Like most are.* She stuffed her hands in her bag and I thought she was rummaging around for a tissue.

'I'm glad you adore your colour, I'm glad you wouldn't ever change it,' she said as her hands came out of her bag, 'but I'd do anything in the world to change mine. Even change it for plain, grim blackness...'

She was holding a small metal cylinder. I recognized what it was instantly. *Kill her, you asshole!*

'...as long as you accompany me.' She held her thumb over the trigger.

I stood up slowly and held my arms out to her. 'Azure, that will kill us both. Why should you die as well?'

'You don't deserve to die, Carmine.'

She pressed the trigger as I hurled myself towards her. The only thing I managed to do was to get myself closer to the explosion. It was a small blast, with just enough strength to scatter minuscule chemical fragments into the room.

I fell on top of her, but it was over. We were alive. I got up and looked at her, puzzled. *What did she do to us?* Azure was smiling. *Look at her blood, Carmine!* She got up and stumbled away from me. She reached the door and felt around. By the time she turned the knob and opened the door, my vision was already blurry and it felt as if small needles were piercing my eyes. At that moment, I realized what had just happened. *See blood! See some blood!*

'Formic fragments, Carmine.'

I could barely make out her shadow.

'They don't kill. They blind. Forever.'

I fell to my knees and tried to see my colour on my forearm. *See the blood!* A giggle escaped my lips. *Scarlet.* I placed my palms in front of my eyes. *Crimson.* I couldn't even make out shadows anymore. *Sanguine.* The needles in my eyes were burning. *This is some kind of relief, Carmine.* I forced myself to remember the colour of blood, but my mind had filled with darkness. *You shouldn't have returned to the city.* This was the only solution. *We should have found another war.* War is my element. *War is blood.*

I lay on the floor and turned face up.

I stayed there until the cops arrived.

*

He approaches as quietly as he can, but not quietly enough.

'Who is it?' The woman's voice is full of pain.

'Detective Asiyar Mohammad.' He opts to use the rank he had when he was in the force.

'Mr. Mohammad, I did it.'

He takes a few steps and reaches the bedside. He can barely make out the familiar features of the woman lying there. Her eyes are covered with bandages. Black flames lick her neck. Her voice is flat. But the old man doesn't need to see all this to know what happened. He knew from the moment Kita had come to his house.

'I found him and I took from him the most precious thing he had.' Her attempt to smile ends with a grimace of pain.

'Calm down, Azure, calm down.'

She swallows with difficulty. 'I took away his colour, and I was released from mine.'

He stretches out his arm and strokes her hair.

But instead of calming, Azure begins to tell him about her adventure, her persistence, her decision; about tattoos, blinding weapons, and night bars with coloured songs. As her story unfolds, he thinks that since '48, when the world became grey, he never searched for his special shade, and a small sting of guilt pinches his soul, as he realises that he is not afraid any more.

He finally knows that he doesn't need a colour just for himself. He knows he's lucky not to have stumbled upon it by chance.

Contributors

Vasso Christou was born in Athens in 1962. She lives in Athens. She has studied Information Technology and works as a teacher in Secondary Education. Her novels, *Λαξευτές της Παλίρροιας* (2006), *Λαξευμένο Δίχτυ* (2007), *Ο Λαξευτής των Στοιχείων* (2009) and her short story collection, *Όλες οι Γεύσεις του Φωτός* (2015), have been published by Ίαμβος Publications. Her short stories have been published in several Greek magazines and anthologies.

Kostas Charitos was born in Arta in 1970. He grew up in Athens, where he currently lives. He studied Chemistry at the University of Patras, where he got his PhD, and works as a teacher in Secondary Education. His short stories have been published in various anthologies and magazines in Greece. His first novel *Σχέδιο Φράκταλ* (*Project Fractal*), was published by Triton Publications in 2009. His second novel *Χαμένα Χρώματα. Κόκκινο* (*Lost colours. Red*) is on print by Kedros Publications. The short story 'Social Engineering' was published in the anthology *a2525* by Science Fiction Club of Athens in 2017.

Ioanna Bourazopoulou was born in Athens in 1968. She has written novels, short stories and plays. Her works have been published in various literary magazines and newspapers. Among her novels is *Τι είδε η Γυναίκα του Λωτ* (*What Lot's Wife Saw*), 2007, Athens Prize for Literature, and listed by *The Guardian* as one of the best science-fiction novels of 2013. She is now writing the trilogy *Ο Δράκος της Πρέσπας* (*The Dragon of Prespa*), the first two volumes of which have been released: - (I) *Η κοιλάδα της λάσπης* (*The valley of Mud*), 2014, Athens Academy Award, Clepsydra magazine Award - (II) *Κεχριμπαρένια Έρημος* (*Amber Desert*, 2019). Other novels: *Το Μπουντουάρ του Ναδίρ* (*The Boudoir of Nadir*), 2003; *Το Μυστικό Νερό* (*The Secret Water*), 2005; *Η Ενοχή της Αθωότητας* (*The Guilt of Innocence*), 2011; the children's book, *Το ταξίδι των τρολ* (*The Journey of the Trols*), 2009.

Michalis Manolios was born in Athens in 1970. His first novel, *Αγέννητοι Αδελφοί*, was published by Κλειδάριθμος Publications in 2014, and his second one, *Το βιβλίο και η περφόρμανς*, by Κέδρος Publications in 2019, while two collections of short stories, *Σάρκινο Φρούτο* and *...και το Τέρας*, have been published by Τρίτων Publications in 1999 and 2009 respectively. His short story 'Aethra', included in the latter, received the Aeon Award in 2010. His short stories have been published in various anthologies and magazines in Greece, Ireland, Italy, the USA, Philippines and China.

Yiannis Papadopoulos is a photographer and video artist by training, digital designer by profession, and an author of science fiction short stories. In 2016 he co-founded *ding: Creative Workshops for Kids*, a workspace designed to promote children's creative thinking & expression through art, design, and storytelling (https://ding.gr). His photographic, video & interactive works have been presented in shows, exhibitions and festivals. His short stories have been published in magazines and anthologies in Greece. The short story *The Bee Problem*, was co-authored with Stamatis Stamatopoulos and published as part of Lina Theodorou's *a2525 Future Athens Stories* art project.

Kelly Theodorakopoulou was born in Athens in 1978, where she studied English Language and Literature. Her short stories have been included in *Μορφές Α* (National and Kapodistrian University of Athens, 2006), *10 Ιστορίες του Φανταστικού* (Archetypo Publications, 2010), *Literary Bistro 2009-2010* (Stella Samiotou Fitzsimons, 2012), *Μαθαίνοντας ποδήλατο* (Κέδρος Publications, 2013), and *ΕΦΦάνταστες Ιστορίες* (ΑΛΕΦ, 2013) anthologies. Her novel, *Η φυλακή στο κεφάλι σου*, was published in 2017 by Comicon Shop Publications.

Eugenia Triantafyllou is a Greek author and artist with a flair for dark things. She currently lives in Athens with a boy and a dog. She is a graduate of Clarion West Writers Workshop. Her short fiction has appeared in *Uncanny, Apex, Strange Horizons, Fireside* and other venues. Find her on Twitter @foxesandroses or her website https://eugeniatriantafyllou.wordpress.com.

Lina Theodorou is a visual artist and a screen writer. She lives and works in Berlin and Athens. She mainly works with videos and installations. She has taken part in several exhibitions, including: the BOZAR Centre for Fine Arts (Brussels), the Vienna Museumsquartier, the National Museum of Contemporary Art (Athens), the EMAF (European Media Art Festival) (Osnabrück), the Deste Foundation (Athens), the Neue Galerie am Landesmuseum Joanneum (Graz), the Museum Fridericianum (Kassel), the State Museum of Contemporary Art (Thessaloniki), the 8th International Biennale, the 6th ev+a Limerick Biennale, the 53rd International Short Film Festival Oberhausen, the 11th International Architecture Exhibition Venice Biennale, the Benaki Museum, (Athens), the Onassis Cultural Centre (Athens), the Biennale of the Moving Image, (Buenos Aires), and so on.

Dimitra Nikolaidou is a PhD researcher at the Aristotle University of Thessaloniki, as well as the head editor at Archetypo Publications and the co-founder of Tales of the Wyrd, a company which organizes creative writing workshops and seminars. Her fiction has appeared in *Beneath Ceaseless Skies*, *Metaphorosis*, *See the Elephant*, *Starship Sofa*, *Gallery of Curiosities* etc as well as in several anthologies (*After the Happily Ever After*, *Retellings of the Inland Seas* etc). Her non-fiction work has been published in *Cracked. com*, *Atlas Obscura*, *Future Skies* etc as well as in several Greek magazines and historical anthologies.

Natalia Theodoridou is a Greek writer and editor, the winner of the 2018 World Fantasy Award for Short Fiction, and a Clarion West graduate (class of 2018). Natalia's stories have appeared in *Clarkesworld, Strange Horizons, Uncanny, Beneath Ceaseless Skies, Nightmare, Fireside,* and *Interzone,* among other venues, and have been translated in Italian, Estonian, Chinese, French, Spanish, and Arabic. *Rent-a-Vice*, Natalia's first interactive novel, was a finalist for the inaugural Nebula Award for Game Writing in 2018. Natalia's latest game, *An Odyssey: Echoes of War,* is published by Choice of Games. For details, visit www.natalia-theodoridou. com or follow @natalia_theodor on Twitter.

Stamatis Stamatopoulos was born in Athens in 1974. His short stories have been published in the *Ελευθεροτυπία* newspaper supplement '9', in *ΕΦΦάνταστες Ιστορίες* (ΑΛΕΦ, 2013), *Εφαρμοσμένη Μυθομηχανική* (sff.gr/press, 2014), *a2525* (ΑΛΕΦ, 2017) and *Αλλόκοσμοι* (Ρενιέρη, 2017) anthologies, and in the *Samovar* magazine (http://samovar.strangehorizons.com/). He lives and works as a carpenter in the UK since 2014. Find him @ RedNirgal on Twitter.

Lightning Source UK Ltd.
Milton Keynes UK
UKHW012127030221
378186UK00003B/149

9 781913 387372